Mary Mae
and the Gospel Truth

Mary Mae
and the Gospel Truth

by Sandra Dutton

HOUGHTON MIFFLIN BOOKS FOR CHILDREN
Houghton Mifflin Harcourt
Boston New York 2010

for Max

Houghton Mifflin Books for Children is an imprint of Houghton Mifflin Harcourt Publishing Company.

www.hmhbooks.com

Epigraph on page v from the essay by Brian Greene "Science Nourishes the Mind and the Soul," copyright © 2005 by Brian Greene, from the book *This I Believe: The Personal Philosophies of Remarkable Men and Women*, edited Jay Allison and Dan Gediman.

The text of this book is set in Dante MT.

Library of Congress Cataloging-in-Publication Data

Dutton, Sandra.
Mary Mae and the Gospel truth / by Sandra Dutton.
p. cm.
Summary: Ten-year-old Mary Mae, living with her parents in fossil-rich southern Ohio, tries to reconcile, despite her mother's strong disapproval, her family's Creationist beliefs with the prehistoric fossils she studies in school.
ISBN 978-0-547-24966-7
[1. Families—Fiction. 2. Mothers and daughters—Fiction. 3. Creationism—Fiction. 4. Christian life—Fiction. 5. Conduct of life—Fiction. 6. Schools—Fiction. 7. Ohio—Fiction.] I. Title.
PZ7.D952Mar 2010
[Fic]—dc22

2009049706

Manufactured in the United States of A
DOC 10 9 8 7 6 5 4 3 2 1
4500229030

Contents

"I've heard they teach the earth is round," Saul said,
"and such a claim goes against Scripture."

—James Still, Sporty Creek

I believe that the breathtaking ideas of science can
nourish not only the mind but also the soul.

—Brian Greene, *"This I Believe," NPR*

1.
Remnant

Stomping, jumping, I'm a-singing away. Me and Granny's up here at the microphone, Granny on guitar, double strumming, foot tapping, urging everyone on for the chorus.

> *"Climb that mountain high and wide,*
> *Jesus keeps you satisfied.*
> *Praise him silly, oh yes.*
> *Praise him silly, oh yes."*

Everybody's clapping. It's a tune Granny wrote herself. I shake the tambourine on the chorus, and Granny ends with a loud "Amen!" She's up here from Crawdad, Kentucky, seeing some doctors about her high blood. We set down with Mama and Daddy, then our pastor, Sister Coates, says it's time for personal testimony. "Who would like to give thanks?"

Jonathan Safer jumps up. "I got a B on my history test."

"Praise the Lord!" Everybody yells. "Amen!"

"I found a good used car," says Roscoe Goodwin. "Got power windows and cruise control."

"Amen! Praise the Lord!"

Granny gets up. "I'm happy to be visiting my family here in DeSailles, Ohio."

"Praise the Lord! Amen!"

Granny's really my great-granny, staying in our old boarder Lucinda's room.

+ + +

I like it here at Remnant. Remnant Church of God. How you can get up and sing and say what you're thankful for. I went to another girl's church, Edna Flotsam's, and we just set quiet on a wooden seat except when we sung songs. And the only time you talked was when you read something out loud.

+ + +

Sister Coates gives her sermon. It's on believing every word of the Bible. She gets all excited, walking back and forth with her microphone, telling us how some people think the Bible is just a bunch of stories, but she's here to tell us it's the solid word of God. "And they got proof over there in the Bible lands that Jesus was there and he done what they said he done." She ends by telling us how we got to spread the word. "It's your duty as a Christian," she says, "to get out and tell other folks about our Lord and Saviour."

She reaches behind the podium and pulls out a box. They's packs of cards in it, wrapped in rubber bands. She holds up one pack and says, "These is John 3:16 stickers. Now what we got to do is get these out to different places. They's fifty in each stack." She pulls one out—it's shiny aluminum, with a cross at the bottom—peels a piece of paper off the back, and sticks it to the front of the podium. "We all know it. Let us recite:

'For God so loved the world
that He gave His only begotten son
that whosoever believeth on Him
should not perish
but have everlasting life.'"

Mama had me memorize that when I was four years old. She says that's the most important verse in the Bible, that you can get to Heaven on that one. And that if you don't, well, you go straight to Hell.

Chloe Sample, she walks right up, takes two stacks, and walks back. Mama's always talking about how full of the spirit Chloe is, throwing her head back during prayer time and falling to the floor. I don't want her to have nothing on me, so I walk up and take three.

"What are some places you can hand these out at?" says Sister Coates. "We got a blessed opportunity to bring folks to the Lord."

Jimmy Toggle says he can hand them out at his factory, Porter Ironworks.

Chloe Sample raises her hand. "I got a White Castle down the street from me," she says.

"Fine place," says Sister Coates.

I want to show Mama I'm just as holy as Chloe. "What about—" I'm trying to think up something grand. "What about—what about going up I-71, and—"

Then Mama gets in the spirit. "We'll do rest stops, Mary Mae. And that big mall up near Chillicothe."

"Praise the Lord," says Sister Coates.

"We can do it next Saturday," Mama whispers.

"I'll be working," says Daddy.

"Then me, Granny, and Mary Mae'll do it," says Mama.

Her giving up Saturday, I know it's important. We're a-saving souls for the Lord.

2.
I-71

Daddy peels the white piece off the back of one of them stickers and puts it on his dashboard.

I take a few to school. Shirley Whirly puts one on her notebook. Weatherford Tatum sticks one on his backpack, and my teacher Miss Sizemore says, "Thank you very much, Mary Mae." But that's all I give out at school. Mostly I can't wait to save the people of Ohio. I picture getting a badge from God for saving the most souls on I-71.

Mama says, "You, me, and Granny can just pepper the restrooms with them signs."

Saturday morning, Mama says be sure and dress warm. It's October and only fifty degrees out. I have on jeans and a navy blue parka. Granny has on her yellow slacks and them sunglasses that stick straight up like an insect.

Mama, she's wearing her black slacks and a sweatshirt that says HARBIN PLUMBING. That's where she works at.

Granny sets up front with Mama, and I set in the back.

"The Lord will have a special place for us," Mama says to Granny and me as we're driving down the highway.

A pickup speeds past doing a hundred.

"Christ Almighty," says Granny.

Mama don't like it when Granny cusses, but she's give up trying to stop it. Says Granny always cussed and there ain't nothing she can do about it. But when I hear Granny say "Christ Almighty," it ain't like she's cussing. It's like she's talking to the Lord.

We pass the exits for Lebanon and Fort Ancient, and by ten o'clock we pull into the Ohio Shops. Parking lot ain't too crowded yet, and we decide to do the main ladies' room off the food court.

"If the stall is empty," says Mama, "put one inside, but make sure it ain't near a coat hook, so it don't get covered up. And if somebody's in there, just put one on the outside of the door."

We each take a stack.

"If we save just one soul," says Mama, "it's worth it."

We're lucky since nobody's in this restroom yet, and we get a sticker up right over each toilet paper roll.

"That way it's bound to get read," says Granny.

Mama buys me a Cinnabon on our way out and gets Granny a cup of coffee. We cross over to the other side of the highway and do the Outlet Mall. They ain't got a food court over there, so we ask the clerk at Donna Fashions where's the biggest restroom. She says it's next to the Ohio Crockery, so we drive down and put stickers there. Put a few on the mirror, too.

"You can't never do too many," says Mama.

Then we cross back and keep heading north.

"Problem is," says Granny, "we ain't taking care of the men."

So Mama, next stop we make, she finds some nice man she thinks she can trust and gets him to put stickers up in the men's room.

By eleven thirty we're at a rest stop just south of Columbus. There's an attendant that wants to know what we're a-doing, and Mama gives her a sticker. "You want to be saved," she says. "Believe on the Lord Jesus, and you'll wind up in Heaven."

This rest stop is busy, so we get only half our stickers inside the stalls. The rest is on the outside of the doors. We hit two more rest stops north of Columbus, going to both sides of the highway, until just about all them stickers is used up. I'm keeping a few, just for emergencies. It's two o'clock.

Mama says, "I think we've earned lunch." We stop at the Cheery Day Diner. Whatever we want, she says. We've earned it.

I get the Cheery Day hamburger platter with free sundae.

Mama gets the tuna melt.

And Granny gets the senior meatloaf special.

I put one of my last stickers on the napkin holder—looks like they was made for each other, both being aluminum—and we head back.

⊹ ⊹ ⊹

Granny and I, we make up a tune to John 3:16.

She goes, "For God so loved"

And I echo, "For God so loved"

> *"He loved the world"*
> > *"He loved the world"*
> *"That he gave"*
> > *"That he gave"*
> *"His only son"*
> > *"His only son"*
> *"That whosoever"*
> > *"Whosoever"*

"Believes on him"
    "Believes on him"
"Shall live"
    "Shall live"
"Forevermore."
    "Forevermore."

And Mama's a-joining in on the echo, and we's just a-rolling down the highway. I look at the speedometer, and we're doing seventy-six—Mama don't usually drive this fast. Then I look behind us and see this car with a red light flashing.

I stop singing. "What's that mean?" I say.

"What?" says Mama.

"That car behind us."

Mama looks in the rearview mirror. "Oh, Jesus Lord."

Mama don't cuss, so I know it must be the highway patrol. She moves onto the shoulder, comes to a full stop.

I see him in his car talking on a radio. It's taking him forever to get out. Finally he walks up. Mama rolls down her window.

"Did you know, ma'am, that you was doing seventy-five in a fifty-five-mile zone?"

"I'm sorry. I didn't realize," says Mama. Her voice don't sound like my mama's at all. She'd been bragging only last week she'd never got a ticket. And been driving for twenty years.

I lean forward through Mama's window. "We're working for the Lord," I say. And I hand him a sticker.

He looks at it, reads it real slow, says to Mama, "You're gonna get to Heaven sooner than you want to if you don't slow down."

I'm wishing I hadn't give him a sticker.

Mama signs some papers, rolls her window back up, and when the highway patrol takes off, she creeps out onto the highway. I look at the speedometer. She's doing forty-five. I'm thinking this is worse than going fast. People are beeping, slamming on their brakes, and pulling around us. We ain't singing no more John 3:16, neither.

"I just didn't realize I was going so fast," says Mama.

She's feeling bad, and me and Granny's being real quiet. I'm setting sideways on the back seat, feet stretched out and my head against the window, thinking that officer might have been doing his duty, but he didn't appreciate what we was doing.

And then I see them stripes Miss Sizemore was talking about at school. They's on a hill that's been cut away for the road. Now I've been down this highway lots of times, but I never seen them stripes before.

"Christ Almighty," I say. Everybody else has been cussing. "Just look at them stripes."

"You don't use that kind of language," Mama says.

"What stripes?" says Granny.

"Remember, Granny? I told you about all them different eras." That's one thing I've been doing since Granny come to visit us. Every day I come home from school, Granny'll say, "What did you learn in school today, Mary Mae?" And I'll tell her.

"Them stripes in the hills," I say. "Shows all the different ages of the earth. You can't see it now. It's way back."

Now Mama's mood just gets worse. "Ain't no different ages," she says.

I don't know what she's talking about. "Why not?" I say.

Mama don't answer right away. She says to Granny, "I swear, them teachers ought to stick with spelling and numbers."

Granny just looks straight ahead. She don't want to get into it with Mama.

"Tempting kids to believe in something that ain't so," Mama goes on. "Just remember what we believe, young lady."

"What do we believe?" I ain't being smart. I just don't know what she's talking about.

"The world is six thousand years old. You look in your Bible."

"Where?"

"Well, Genesis. Where else? You got the whole Creation, right there."

⊹ ⊹ ⊹

Soon as we get home, I get my Bible out and run my finger down every line of Genesis. I'm looking for six thousand, whether it's in numbers or spelled out in letters. I go through twice. Second time I'm reading with a flashlight in bed. Only six I find is on the "sixth day," what God created, and in different folks' ages, like Enoch living three hundred and *sixty*-five years.

I tell Mama Sunday morning I can't find no six thousand, and she says she don't have time to look, she's got too much work to do.

"What do you think, Granny?" I ask at breakfast. "Do you think the world is only six thousand years old?"

"It's whatever the Lord made it," says Granny.

3.
Puppet Show

Sister Coates is a-standing in the middle of the church basement where we have Sunday school, and I decide to ask her. "Whereat in the Bible does it say the world is six thousand years old?"

She looks up a second, like she ain't been asked that question before, then says, "Well, it don't come right out and say this. It's implied."

"What's that mean?"

"It means something is suggested without coming right out and saying it. Like if you put two and two together," she says, "you'll come up with four."

I shake my head. I still don't understand.

"We got to pay attention to Bible scholars that say when they count the generations—and a generation is twenty years—that Adam and Eve was created six thousand years ago. That's the implication. It's that many generations mentioned in the Bible."

"Oh," I say.

Sister Coates goes on. "You know where it says 'begat'? Like Abraham begat Isaac and Isaac begat Jacob and Esau?"

"You mean if I count each begat, I'll come up with six thousand years?"

"You got to multiply by twenty," says Sister Coates. "That's a generation." She looks at me real concerned, then says, "Mary Mae, I think you could use some special study of the Creation. I'm a-talking to Brother Lucas."

He's my Sunday school teacher.

I walk over to the junior corner, where my Sunday school class meets at nine o'clock. We got our banner hanging there: JUNIORS 1988–89. I'd like to start counting begats right now, but I ain't got a pencil. Besides, I got to pay attention in class. Orlin Coates, Sister Coates's son's there, and so's Chloe. She's reading her Bible, and her hair's spread all over her shoulders like a waterfall. It's blond, almost white, and Mama says she looks just like an angel. Mama's always saying to me, when she plaits my hair, "Why don't we let it hang loose, like Chloe's?"

"I don't want to look like Chloe," I tell her.

Me, Chloe, and Orlin set and wait, and then three more in our class come—Jed Bean, Chester Morley, and Jonathan Safer. We got all boys except for Chloe and me.

Brother Lucas—him and Sister Coates is still a-going at it, talking, nodding, Brother Lucas making notes.

Finally he comes over. "Sister Coates and I," he says, handing out our Sunday school paper, "we was talking about how important it is to know the Creation. And we was thinking you might like to do a puppet show."

Puppet show? We all look at each other.

"She wants us to do Genesis—Creation, Temptation, and Noah's Ark. For the church potluck next month."

"How can you do a puppet show on Creation?" I say. "Don't seem to me there's no need for puppets."

"Let's take a look," says Brother Lucas. We all open up our Bibles to chapter 1 and go around the class reading each verse, how God separates the light from the dark and the land from the water and goes on to making fruit trees and winged fowl. And then I'm a-reading on verse 26:

> "And God said, Let us make man in our image,
> after our likeness."

"That's the first place we need puppets," I say. "So what are we going to do up to this verse?"

"Anyone got any ideas?" says Brother Lucas.

"Just do God's voice," says Orlin.

"And we could turn on a light when God says, 'Let there be light!'" says Chester.

"Flashlight," says Jonathan.

"I know!" says Chloe. "We could paint a backdrop for each day."

"Yeah," says Orlin. "'Let there be mountains,' and boom, this backdrop comes down."

"And we could do some thunder," says Jed. "Get a piece of sheet metal and rattle it."

"Just use puppets for Adam and Eve and Noah's Ark," says Jonathan.

"Good idea," says Brother Lucas. "Sounds like you'd like to do it." He looks at me. "What do you think, Mary Mae?"

I don't want to come around too quick, especially with Brother Lucas and Sister Coates thinking they can teach me a lesson. But truth to tell, it sounds like a whole lot more fun than what we usually do, which is read our Sunday school paper. "Do we get to keep the puppets?" I say.

"I don't see why not," says Brother Lucas.

"You can keep mine, too," says Chester Morley. He's making puppy sounds, squishing the air out between his palms.

"I wouldn't want yours," I say. Then to Brother Lucas I say, "Why ain't we doing Cain and Abel?"

"Sister Coates says we only got time for three scenes," says Brother Lucas.

"Then why not Creation, Temptation, and Cain and Abel."

"Noah's Ark's got more to do with Creation."

I think about it a minute. I got the whole class waiting for me to say yes. "Okay," I say. "I'd like to do it."

Brother Lucas nods. "Who knows how to make a puppet stage?"

"It's easy," says Orlin. "All you do is get three big pieces of plywood. Put hinges and cut a window in the middle. We made one at school."

"I can get some plywood from my neighbor," says Brother Lucas. "How about us meeting at my house Tuesday night to make the stage?"

"I go to Scouts," says Orlin.

"How about Wednesday?"

"Wednesday's good for me," says Chloe. Turns out it's good for everybody else, so we decide to meet at seven at Brother Lucas's house on Charter Street.

✠ ✠ ✠

During service, me and Granny sing "Light Me Lord, I'm Full of Glory." That's another one of Granny's tunes.

Sister Coates wants to know did everyone get their stickers out. Chloe says she stood in front of White Castle and handed hers out. Dudley Rayburn pasted his all up and down the main street of St. Bevis. Jaber and Wilma Tatters say they just didn't have time and would get to handing theirs out next week. Me, Mama, and Granny tell how we hit all the malls and rest stops. Mama even confesses to getting a speeding ticket.

"Lord's way of keeping you safe," says Sister Coates. She winks. "Praise Jesus. Now who wants to give thanks this morning?"

Chester Morley leaps up. "I got a new paper route."

Evelyn Mognis raises her hand. "I won a year's supply of free laundry soap." She don't like to stand since she's got a bad back.

"Hallelujah! Praise the Lord!"

Buford Safer, Jonathan's daddy, says, "I'm grateful my foot surgery was successful."

✠ ✠ ✠

This morning Sister Coates preaches on the Ten Commandments. "Some folks think they don't apply, but they're as good today as they was for the people of Moses. And I want you to pay special attention to the fifth commandment, Exodus 20:12, 'Honor thy father and thy mother.'

You got to be respectful and do what they tell you to do. Don't give them no sass." She winks at Orlin, then tells stories about kids that was a credit to their mama and daddy, pulling out chairs and opening doors, leaving some orange juice in the carton for the next person. Before she closes, she says, "Brother Lucas, is it true the junior class is doing a puppet show on Creation?"

"Next month," says Brother Lucas.

"Something we can all look forward to," says Sister Coates.

⊹ ⊹ ⊹

We're driving home, and Mama's all excited about my doing puppets. "You'll learn the true Creation this way," she says. "Get rid of all them silly ideas you're learning at school."

At home I go upstairs and start putting a check mark on each begat. I'm running a tally at the front of my Bible.

4.
Digging

I come in to school early Monday, and Miss Sizemore's setting at the desk eating sliced peaches from a plastic cup.

"Good morning," she says.

"Morning," I say.

She's got red hair, short, like she don't want to mess with it. I think about telling her my mama and Sister Coates say the world ain't but six thousand years old, but I ain't counted all the begats yet. Besides, I'm wondering how a generation can be twenty years, when all them Bible people's having kids when they's more than a hundred years old. I got to ask Sister Coates about this.

I set down, put my lunch away. Then I look at Miss Sizemore's charts. Besides the one with the cutaway hill, she's got a big, tall one with all them eras. It's right up the side of the room. Dinosaurs come 250 million years ago, but the bottom of the chart goes all the way back to 4,000 million years. I can't hardly figure out how far back that is. It's like reaching into a sock and finding no toe.

I'm thinking it would be a whole lot easier if the world was only six thousand years old. But maybe it ain't.

⊹ ⊹ ⊹

Herschel Cadwallader comes in. He's got some shells he found in his own backyard. Miss Sizemore has Herschel make labels and put them on display. He sets right across from me.

Soon as everybody's in and we've did the pledge and collected the lunch money, Miss Sizemore points on the chart to the Ordovician age. It's the purple box. She says it once and has us repeat it. *Or-do-vish'-e-un.* "That's five hundred million years ago," she says. "Right here in southern Ohio, during the Ordovician age, this land was covered with a warm, shallow sea." Just imagine you was alive at that time, she says. There was palm fronds, and we was twenty degrees north of the equator.

That's what I like about Miss Sizemore. She makes a story out of things.

"You would be one of the early forms of life," she says. "You might be a trilobite." She writes it on the board,

tRiLobite

Then she says there was different kinds of trilobites, but the one we had the most of right here in southern Ohio was the *Flexicalymene*. She writes that on the board, too.

If you was a trilobite, she says, you probably growed from an egg. And you would be crawling around on the bottom of the sea. "You would be a distant relative of the crab."

Miss Sizemore shows us a picture. "You have three main parts. That's why you're called *tri*lobite, because *tri*- means three. And you have little cross grooves so you can roll into a ball. There's a special word for that. It's *enroll*. Now why do you think a trilobite would roll into a ball?"

"For protection?" says Herschel Cadwallader.

"Just like a pill bug," says Miss Sizemore. She shows us some more pictures of trilobites, all sizes, some of them enrolled, and says there was millions of trilobites for millions and millions of years.

We all look at each other.

Shirley Whirly leans across the aisle. "She don't know what she's talking about. The world ain't that old." Shirley goes to Calvary Temple.

But I want to hear Miss Sizemore out.

"We're lucky, living in southern Ohio," Miss Sizemore says, "because it's one of the best places to hunt for fossils. We have what's called the Cincinnati Arch." She draws a picture up on the board, with a big old arch a-pushing up through the layers. "The new rock has been worn away, exposing the older rock from the Ordovician age." She says this don't happen in most places. In most places the old rock stays buried.

Me and Herschel look at each other like we's learning important secrets. Shirley Whirly, setting behind Herschel, stares up at the ceiling.

Miss Sizemore hands each of us a xerox—"Southern Ohio Fossils." Most of them look like seashells you'd find on a beach.

She tells us how them fossils was made. Long ago, when one of them sea animals died, its inside rotted out and limestone drifted in. The limestone got hard, and the shell broke off, so what you have is what you get when you pour plaster of Paris into a mold.

"We'll be digging for fossils right here in our school yard," says Miss Sizemore.

Right away I know where she's taking us. They's building a new addition onto our school where the old primary playground used to be, and the hole was just dug last week. She says the principal told her they ain't a-coming back till next Monday.

"I'll bring shovels," says Miss Sizemore, "but I want each of you to have a hammer and chisel. Or you can bring a screwdriver." She writes on the board

hammer
chisel or screwdriver

"I'm dividing you into groups." She puts me with Shirley Whirly and Herschel Cadwallader.

✛ ✛ ✛

When Granny asks me what we learned in school today, I tell her all about trilobites and how southern Ohio was right down by the equator. "We're digging for fossils tomorrow, too," I tell her.

"Wish I could dig for fossils," says Granny. "But I'm just an old fossil myself."

✛ ✛ ✛

After dinner I ask Daddy if I can borrow a hammer and chisel.

"What do you need them for?" he asks.

"We're digging," I say. I don't say nothing about fossils. Don't want to stir up no trouble.

"Digging?" says Daddy. "You know when I was in school we didn't go out digging. We stayed inside and learned our lessons."

✠ ✠ ✠

Herschel Cadwallader brings in his hammer and chisel, but Shirley Whirly don't bring nothing. She goes right up to Miss Sizemore. "Mama told me I ain't allowed to dig," she says.

"She afraid you'll get dirty?" says Miss Sizemore.

"No, digging goes against my religion."

I'm thinking Miss Sizemore might try and talk Shirley into it, but she just says, "All right, you can be in charge of labeling," and gives her a box and a pencil with some stick 'ems.

Shirley comes back to her seat.

"Whereat in the Bible does it say we ain't allowed to dig?" I ask her.

"Mama says the Lord don't mind us digging, long as we're just planting seeds. But we go digging for things that ain't in the Bible and we're asking for trouble."

✥ ✥ ✥

Miss Sizemore hands out goggles so we don't get our eyes hurt. We look like scuba divers. Whole class walks down the steps and into where the old primary playground was. They had a ditch digger come and chew right through the blacktop. Got a big pile of dirt up by the street. You can walk into the hole from one side, so we go in and kneel by some big slabs of rock. Miss Sizemore says they's shale and limestone. And they's just a-teeming with all kinds of shells.

✥ ✥ ✥

Shirley Whirly sets on the edge of a rock, her shoes banging against the side.

I know Mama would be proud of me if I set with Shirley, but truth to tell, I can't wait to see what I can turn up. It's like a treasure hunt.

Me and Herschel's chipping away on one of them

slabs. You got to chip real careful to get a piece out. Everyone's excited. Our whole class, we's spread out over the hole like a bunch of carpenter ants. One group chips a whole bunch of crinoids loose—them's little sea plants with dots like goose bumps—and another group brings out some clams and a starfish. Me and Herschel chip out some coral, and I find a long, fat point that Miss Sizemore says come from a squid. We give them to Shirley. She puts our names on them. When we go back into the building, we clean all them fossils up with some old toothbrushes and put them on a table for display.

But every time I walk by that window, I want to get out and dig. Can't wait to see what I can turn up.

Herschel, too. We go out after school. Don't even need a shovel. Just our hammers and chisels. We find a good slab, and Herschel's working to bring up a starfish. I got this little round animal with ridges I'm working on. Want to bring it up whole. Dust is flying up, and my fingernails is getting dirty. Herschel gets himself all but one point of the starfish. "Wow!" he says. "I'm putting this in my collection."

"Collection?" I say. "What kind of collection?"

"Things I find. Daddy got me a cabinet with glass doors. Every time I find something, I put it in there—arrowheads, fossils, bird feathers. I love collecting things."

"Me, too," I say. And I'm thinking, I'll get me a box. Something to keep all my fossils in. I'll have a *collection*.

I'm cracking all around these ridges, and pieces is falling away, and what do you know, I find this funny-looking animal. "Look at this," I say to Herschel. Looks sort of like a pill bug, all rolled up. It's an inch and a half, just like one of them pictures Miss Sizemore give us.

"Wow," he says, "you got a trilobite."

"Think so?" I'd love it to be a trilobite. I wrap it up in notebook paper and put it in my backpack.

＋ ＋ ＋

Granny's wondering where I've been.

"Digging," I say, and I show her my fossil.

"Lordy, look at that," she says. She picks it up. "Looks like a little crab. Look at them eyes."

"Little bitty eyes," I say. They's sticking out of each side of his head. "Me and Herschel think he's a trilobite."

"Ohhh," says Granny. I told her all about them yesterday.

I take a pen with an old-time point to pick off all the grit, and an old toothbrush to clean him up good. I wrap him in an old sock so I can show him to Miss Sizemore.

Then I find a cigar box down in the cellar. Whenever I find new fossils, I'll put them in here. This will be my collection. I take it up to my room and set it on my dressing table. It's an old wood dressing table with arms that pull out and a drawer inside.

✤ ✤ ✤

Next day I show that little animal to Miss Sizemore. Herschel comes in early with me.

"Oh my," she says. She puts down her cinnamon crisp and wipes her hands. "Mary Mae, you've found a trilobite."

"See, I told you," says Herschel.

And when the whole class is in, she has them gather around.

My trilobite ain't got no legs, only just the shell that was made from the limestone. But it looks just like a real animal to me.

After school, me and Herschel go out and dig some more. He finds some horned coral, and I find some crinoids and a giant snail.

✤ ✤ ✤

When I get home, I show them to Granny. "And you know what, Granny, that little animal I found yesterday really was a trilobite." She starts picking out a tune on her guitar.

> "Trilobite crab, trilobite crab,
>   He don't need no taxicab.
>   Critter and a swimmer from another age.
>   Don't need a tank and he don't need a cage."

Then she hands me her guitar—she's been showing me how to do chords—and I pick out some more words:

> "Trilobite crab, trilobite crab,
>   Little bitty eyes and a nose like a scab.
>   Rolls in a ball like a little pill bug.
>   Swims in the water and he sings, 'Glub, glub.'"

"Hey, we just made up a song," I say.

"That's how you do it," says Granny. "If you work too hard at it, it won't work. You just gotta let it bubble up."

5.
Mrs. Noah

Mama drops me off at Brother Lucas's Wednesday night. He's got a swing on his porch and a big old knocker on the front door. His wife gives us some Hi Ho crackers with grape jelly and fruit punch. Everybody's here but Jonathan Safer. He's got a cold. We go downstairs to Brother Lucas's cellar and all take turns standing next to one of the plywood boards so we can figure out where to cut the hole—not too high for some, not too low for others. Him and Orlin measure down six inches and draw a big rectangle, then we each take turns putting on goggles and cutting the hole with Brother Lucas's jigsaw.

Feels like it could rattle right out of my hand.

We put the three pieces flat out on the floor and hinge them together. Then Brother Lucas gives us some old draw drapes we can use on the opening, and we screw them on.

Jed Bean and Chester Morley don't help much, just go

riding around the cellar on Brother Lucas's son's kiddie car. It's me, Orlin Coates, and Chloe doing all the work.

"All right, next we got to list the parts for the play," says Brother Lucas. He writes on a piece of cardboard.

God
Adam & Eve
The Devil

"I'm God," says Orlin. Him being the tallest and the pastor's son, we don't argue.

"I get to be Eve," says Chloe, fluffing out her hair.

"Hey, wait a minute," I say. "There ain't no more girl's parts."

"You could be the Devil," says Chester Morley.

"Maybe I will," I say.

"No, I'm the Devil," says Jed Bean.

"Settle down," says Brother Lucas. He writes two more parts on the board.

Noah
Mrs. Noah

"I think Mary Mae should be Mrs. Noah," says Brother Lucas.

"She didn't do nothing," I say.

"Yes, she did," says Brother Lucas. "She was in charge of the animals."

I'm thinking he's making this up, just to give me something to do, but I always did like Noah's ark. I had me a cardboard one with little plastic animals I used to march around in the dirt. "But how are we doing all them animals?" I say. "I don't want to be in charge of a hundred puppets."

"You draw them on the backdrop," says Brother Lucas.

Oh yes, backdrop. All them animals marching into the ark.

And then Brother Lucas says, "Chester Morley, I want you to be Noah."

Oh no. I'm Chester Morley's wife. Him and his penguin walk. I'd lock myself in a closet before I'd marry Chester.

Brother Lucas writes all our names on the cardboard, then gets a paper bag and pulls out some big old blocks of wood with the ends all narrowed down. "This here's balsa wood," he says. "Nice and light. They's got a finger hole drilled." He sticks his finger up one. "You can carve out a face—or just paint one on if you can't carve—glue on some yarn for hair, attach a body. Get your mama or daddy to help you."

Since Orlin, being God, don't have to make a puppet, Brother Lucas says he can help Jonathan Safer make Adam.

"You boys and girls bring these puppets in next Sunday," says Brother Lucas.

Orlin Coates takes Brother Lucas's empty bag and pulls it over his head. "God here. I think I'll make me a universe."

And then, I don't know why, I just can't stop myself, I say, "Is this really the way God done it?" I'm the only one in my Sunday school class that goes to DeSailles North, the only one that has Miss Sizemore.

"What do you mean, Mary Mae?" says Brother Lucas.

"Did God really make the world the way it says in the Bible?"

Orlin Coates pulls the bag off his head, crosses his arms like a school principal. "Mary Mae, I'm surprised at you."

"The Bible is God's holy word," says Chloe, and she's glancing from me to Brother Lucas, shaking her hair all over her shoulders, looking at me like I'm lost to Hell.

Jed Bean and Chester Morley ain't paying no attention, just pretend fighting with yardsticks.

"Mary Mae, this puppet show has a purpose," says Brother Lucas.

Orlin's folding the paper bag up all perfect, like he never had it on his head. "It's to show us the true Creation," he says.

✠ ✠ ✠

Mama picks me up and wants to hear all about the making of the puppet stage. "We didn't do nothing like that when I was in Sunday school," she says.

We get home, and she finds an old yellow and white checked apron, says I can use it for Mrs. Noah.

"They didn't have checks in them days," I say.

"How do you know?" says Mama.

"Because I seen the pictures. They weared stripes, like Joseph's coat of many colors."

"We don't have no stripes," says Mama, "so you're just going to have to use this." Mama don't like buying things she don't have to. She runs up a yellow checked puppet's body on her portable sewing machine.

"Looks like a housewife," I say.

"That's exactly what she was," says Mama. "Now get you some hair and paint on a face, and you'll have you a real nice puppet."

Only color yarn I can find up in the attic is blue, so I

glue it on, but I don't know how to carve, so I just paint on a face with poster paint. I do a pink mouth, orange cheeks, and purple eyes.

And I set Mrs. Noah on a pop bottle on my dressing table.

6.
Day by Day

Sunday, Brother Lucas brings the puppet stage to church in the back of his pickup. The boys go out and carry it in, and we set it up in the junior corner.

Chloe pulls Eve out of a shopping bag, holds her up. She's got two big red titties with sparkles in the middle.

"Got these off my mama's coat," says Chloe.

Chester Morley whistles.

"Shut up," says Chloe.

Then he looks at Mrs. Noah. "Ew, blue hair."

"Looks better than yours," I say.

Chester's glued on some carpet padding for Noah's hair, looks like a thatched roof, and his coat's made from a dirty dishtowel.

Jonathan Safer don't have Adam done yet, since he wasn't there Wednesday. And Orlin Coates didn't help him none by working on it at home. Just hands him the block of wood. But Jed Bean done up the Devil like a real artist. Carved out a snake's head with its mouth open and glued in a long red tongue. Had to add him another finger hole, too, since the snake's head needs to set sideways, not straight up and down. He done it with his daddy's drill. Then the rest of the snake's body is made from old pajamas with a red and blue diamond pattern.

Brother Lucas brings in a box of permanent Magic Markers and an old sheet ripped up so we can do the backdrops.

"We'll just draw what God done," says Brother Lucas, "except for Day One. We don't need to draw nothing, since God just separated the light from the dark. We'll use a flashlight and this here backdrop." He takes out a bamboo pole with some black cheesecloth stapled onto it and puts it across the back of the puppet theatre.

Orlin and Jed, they draw Day Two, where God separates the water from the sky. Chester Morley, him and Jonathan Safer do Day Three, making plants and trees. Me and Chloe, we're doing Day Four, where God makes the sun, moon, and stars. But I start thinking, How did God separate the light from the dark on Day One if he didn't make the sun, moon, and stars till Day Four?

I ask Brother Lucas.

"Mary Mae, if God wants to separate something before he makes it, that's his privilege. Don't go asking questions. This is the *Bible,* Mary Mae."

"Maybe it was a different kind of light God made on Day One," says Orlin, trying to play Brother Lucas.

"You mean he made some infrared rays?" I say.

"Maybe there was glow-in-the-dark rocks," says Chester Morley.

"There wasn't no rocks till Day Three," I say.

"Mary Mae, you got to have faith," says Chloe. She looks at Brother Lucas to make sure he heard, then fluffs out her angel hair.

Jed Bean moves on to Day Five, making sea monsters and fish and birds. He's good at that. The rest of us color them in. Orlin's doing Day Six, drawing a lot of animals.

Them Magic Markers is making the junior corner smell like a paint factory.

We attach each of them pictures to a bamboo stick with a staple gun, and then we roll them up and rest them across the top of the puppet stage. Orlin hammers in some nails between each stick to keep them separate. So we got Days One to Six all lined up. Don't need no Day Seven, since God didn't do nothing but rest. Brother Lucas asks who would like to be in charge of the backdrops.

Ain't nobody wants to do it, so I say I will. All you got to do is pull down each day.

Meantimes, Chester and me's supposed to draw the ark, but we ain't good at animals. Jed Bean helps us out by copying a picture Brother Lucas give us. It's got all them animals marching into the ark, but while he's outlining the elephant, I start thinking again. "What about dinosaurs?" I say. "They got to be on the ark."

"Mary Mae, the Bible don't have no dinosaurs," says Chloe, real loud so Brother Lucas can pat her on the head.

"Bible talks about beasts," I say.

"Well, yes," says Brother Lucas. "It does." He takes a breath, heaves it out. "You go ahead and put them in," he says to Jed.

I start thinking about trilobites, too, but since they was in the water, I know we don't got to worry about them.

So Jed Bean puts two *Tyrannosaurus rex*es behind the elephants. Me and Chester color them in, but we're running out of time, so Brother Lucas says we'll have to finish next week.

We put the Magic Markers away. But I start thinking about bugs and insects. "Where are we going to put them insects?" I ask Brother Lucas. I'm following him up the stairs to the main hall with Granny's guitar.

"Why are you so worried about insects?"

"Lord made insects, too," I say. "They got a whole building full at the zoo."

Brother Lucas sighs again. "Mary Mae, you read Genesis. Bible says the ark is three hundred cubits long."

"What's a cubit?"

"Cubit's a *forearm*." He says it like it's something any dumb-dumb would know. "Point is, the ark was one and a half football fields long. Now that's a pretty big ship. Noah for sure would have had enough room for insects."

"But insects don't stay where you put them," I say. "They crawl around. Or fly. And insects eat other insects. How are we going to keep all them insects separate?"

"Maybe they was in little tiny cages."

I'm wondering what them cages was made of, but you can tell Brother Lucas don't want to talk no more. "Mary Mae," he says, "the Lord performs miracles. You got to remember this is a holy expedition." And he goes up the aisle and sets with his wife.

I just want to know things. It seems to me the Bible ain't giving the whole story. How was all them animals fed? That's what I'd like to know. Most all of them eats something different, and there wouldn't hardly be room enough to hold all their food. I done been to the library at school.

Couldn't find nothing. Just pretty picture books with Noah a-standing there and all them animals marching in. Nobody goes inside and tells how they done it. So I'm thinking maybe the Lord was dropping food down onto the ark hisself. Like he give free food to the children of Israel.

✛ ✛ ✛

Granny and I sing "Devil's Got Your Number," only this time I play guitar and she plays fiddle.

Sister Coates asks who would like to give thanks.

"I'm grateful I got a dollar per hour raise," says Chester Morley's mama.

"I'm glad I don't have to move to Tampa," says Billy Grover.

"My gardenias is coming into full bloom," says Wanda Brierly. "Laundry room smells like a perfumery, and I got six new buds."

"Praise Jesus," says Sister Coates.

✛ ✛ ✛

She preaches on the third commandment, Exodus 20:7: "Thou shalt not take the name of the Lord thy God in vain."

I can tell Mama's real pleased that Granny's getting this lesson. She's saying "Amen" and "Oh yes" to everything Sister Coates is a-saying. But after benediction Granny can't find her glasses and cusses up a storm.

"Granny!" says Mama.

"Sweet Jesus," says Granny, "I apologize!"

✠ ✠ ✠

Before we leave, I got to talk to Sister Coates. "How can you count each generation twenty years when some of them Bible people didn't have kids till they was ninety years old?"

"Mary Mae, all I can say is, you got to trust the Bible scholars. They been adding up them numbers longer than we have."

"But I like to add them up myself."

Sister Coates nods, like she understands, but her eyebrows is a-going up at the same time, like she wishes I would quit.

"I got another question," I say. "Who wrote the Bible?"

Sister Coates takes a deep breath and looks at her watch. "Bible was wrote by God, but he was dictating to a lot of folks," she says. "They wrote on scrolls and stored them in pots."

"Do you think things was left out when they was copying?" I ask.

"Oh, they was pretty careful," says Sister Coates.

But I ain't so sure.

7.
Questions

Mary Mae, sit down here," says Mama.

It's Sunday afternoon. She points to the seat on the other side of the table. I know something's coming on.

"I been meaning to talk to you." She takes a sip of her soda. "Sister Coates says you've been asking a lot of questions."

"She likes questions," I say. "She says if we got any, just ask."

"There are things you should not question." Mama slides her glass to the side, sets her elbow on the table, and talks with her pointer finger. "You do not question the Lord's plan. You do not question the Lord's grace. You do not question the Lord's word."

"Why not?"

"What do you mean, why not?" Mama looks around the room like she can't believe I'm questioning her. "Mary Mae, Satan has come and had a heyday in your head."

Right away I'm thinking of Jed Bean's Devil puppet, how it's setting right under my forehead. "I just like to know things, that all."

"All you need to know is right on that sticker we put up, John 3:16. You do not need to know about generations. You do not need to know *why* the Lord done anything. He has his reasons. If you're learning things at school that don't mesh with the Bible, you got to tell your teacher you ain't allowed to hear it. She'll have to give you another assignment."

"I don't want no other assignments. I want to do what everybody else does."

"I'm warning you, Mary Mae, if you're learning things that ain't in line with what we believe, I'll have to take you out of school."

"You can't do that."

"Yes I can. I'll teach you at home."

"But it ain't legal."

"Oh yes it is. I read about it in *Christian Testament*."

Mama goes and gets her magazine. It's opened up to a picture of a mama and two kids setting at a table. Mama starts reading. "'I just did not like what was being taught in the schools,' says Mrs. DeVries, 'and I discovered it is my right as a parent to educate my children at home.'"

"Hmmph," I say. "I don't want to stay at home. All I'd get is Bible and spelling."

"That's all you need," says Mama. "That and a little bit of numbers. Now I don't want to do that. Lord knows, I got enough to do down at Harbin Plumbing. But I got to be certain you're being brought up Bible. Why can't you be my sweet little Mary Mae? It's all so easy if you just believe what the Bible says and don't go asking no questions. Mary Mae, you got to be a witness for others. Like what we done last Saturday, spreading the message of the Lord."

"I do want to spread the message," I say. "I want everybody to go to Heaven. But I want to know things, too. Like how come the ground's all set down in stripes? And how come there's all them little animals in the rocks around here?"

Mama goes over to the refrigerator for more ice. "What little animals?"

"They's seashells around here because this used to be an ocean. One kid even found a trilobite." I don't tell her who.

"What's that?" says Mama.

"It's a little animal used to live a long time ago."

"Is it mentioned in the Bible?"

"I don't think so."

"Well if it ain't in the Bible it ain't a real animal."

"But lots of things ain't in the Bible."

"If you ask me," says Mama, taking a sip of soda, "the Lord put all them shells in the ground just to trick us."

"Trick us?"

"Folks that don't believe in the Bible think the world's older than six thousand years. It's the Lord's test."

But if Mama's right, the Lord had to mix up a whole lot of dirt all different colors and drop them shells in like nuts in cookie batter. And why would he want to do that? Why would the Lord that loves us want to play tricks?

So I ask Miss Sizemore next day before school, "Do you think the Lord put all them shells in the rocks just to make us *think* the world's old?" I feel a little silly asking, because it makes the Lord sound like a cardsharp.

"The world is old," says Miss Sizemore. "What you see on the chart is only the life of the earth. The universe goes back billions of years."

A loud whoosh goes through my head when I hear the word billions. "How do they know?" I ask.

"By measuring the light from the stars. Scientists have determined that the stars are moving away from us."

"But how do they know that?"

"They measure something called a red shift. Even on

earth, light moving away from us creates a red shift. Measuring this, they can calculate speed and count backwards."

"How far back?" I say.

"Fifteen billion years."

I gulp. "But what was the beginning? What was it like at the beginning?"

"One particle. That's what scientists believe. That it exploded, and just kept expanding."

"Sort of like something from nothing?"

"That's right," says Miss Sizemore.

Sounds like Creation to me. I walk over to my seat. One minute I picture the Lord popping out of that particle like a genie. The next minute I picture him holding the particle.

✠ ✠ ✠

I tell Granny about the world being billions and billions of years old. "So how come the Bible says Creation took six days?" I say.

"Maybe days was longer back then," she says. "Maybe a day was billions of years."

"But I'm a-wondering when Noah's ark was," I say.

"Don't seem to me it matters," says Granny. "Time ain't something we can pin down that good."

⊹ ⊹ ⊹

Me and Herschel go out one more day after school. It's the last chance we got, since they's coming back to do the foundation. I find some brachiopods and a spiny snail.

"Think you could come with me and hunt for fossils next Saturday?" says Herschel.

"I don't think so," I say. "I ain't even supposed to be here."

"Why not?"

"Mama thinks digging's bad. She wants me to get other assignments."

"You mean like Shirley Whirly?"

I nod. "Says if I don't, she's taking me out of school."

⊹ ⊹ ⊹

Later I'm setting in my room at my dressing table studying my collection, got my fossils lined up in front of Mrs. Noah. I'm a-cleaning them up with a toothbrush and don't hear Mama come up the stairs.

"Mary Mae, you can't have rocks up here."

"These ain't rocks," I tell her.

"What are they?" She picks up a coral, turns it around.

I'm thinking of making something up, but instead I just come out with it. "Fossils."

"Fossils? Well you get them things out of here. I'm warning you you're headed for homeschooling." Mama drops the coral into my cigar box. "You get them things out to the trash."

I put the other fossils back in my cigar box. I start to follow Mama downstairs, but instead I open up the arms to my dressing table and hide my cigar box in the back of my drawer.

8.
Report

Miss Sizemore says she wants us to write a report—two pages on one of the fossils we've been studying. We're skipping dinosaurs, she says, since southern Ohio don't have no dinosaur fossils. They come after the Ordovician age, and all them layers was wore off.

Shirley Whirly raises her hand and reminds Miss Sizemore she ain't allowed to write on fossils. Miss Sizemore says she can write on Ohio Valley weather instead. "Is there anyone else whose parents do not want them to report on fossils?" she asks.

Herschel looks at me. I don't raise my hand. I want to learn as much about trilobites as I can. I ask Miss Sizemore if I can do a report on them like an interview. Good idea, she says. So I do some reading, and this is what I write:

MM: Tell us how you spend your day, Mr. Trilobite.
T: Well, I mostly nose around in the bottom and eat.

MM: What do you eat?
T: I have worms sometimes. I walk along until I find a worm trail. Then I just wait for them.

MM: Then what do you do?
T: I sit around in the mud some more. Then I do some swimming. Sometimes I molt.

MM: What does that mean, Mr. Trilobite?
T: Means my shell comes off and I go around unprotected until I grow a new one. That's how I get bigger. I bust out of my old suit and grow me a new one.

MM: How big can you get?
T: I got a cousin that's eight inches. Me, I'm only an inch and a half.

MM: Mr. Trilobite, do you have any enemies?
T: Yes, I do.

MM: Tell us who they are.
T: Cephalopods.

MM: What are cephalopods, Mr. Trilobite?
T: Squids.

MM: Are you able to defend yourself?
T: I got a few things I can do, like roll into a ball. A squid can still eat me, but I'm not as tasty that way. I can swim into a cave, too. And I can sit with a lot of other trilobites.

Then I got a lot of other questions I ain't got the answers to, but I put them down to find out later.

Do trilobites have families?
Do trilobites have houses, like a hole in the sand?
Do trilobites ever fight with each other?
Do trilobites ever sleep?

I take this home and read it to Granny. Then me and her make up some more verses to our trilobite song.

Trilobite crab, trilobite crab,
Who's his mom and who's his dad?
Eats up worms, then rolls in a ball
Hides from the squid with the big eyeball.

Trilobite crab, trilobite crab.
Rolls in the mud and likes to gab.
Cracks his suit, that's how he grows.
Molts his shell from head to toes.

We put them all together with the verses we made up last week, and we sing away.

✠ ✠ ✠

Tonight Mama and Granny are setting down at the kitchen table, and Mama gets to talking about our boarder Lucinda that went back to Clarksville, Indiana. She don't come right out and say it, but I know what she's a-coming around to. Lucinda, that never had no boyfriends, up and got pregnant, and went back home to have her baby, only Mama don't want me to know.

So now, today, she says, "Mary Mae, I don't think this is for your ears. You better get yourself upstairs."

"I don't want to go upstairs," I say. "I'm old enough."

"No, you ain't, and you better do what I say. You got homework to do."

"I already done it."

Then Mama brings her hand down and says, "Now."

I look at Granny and she just smiles.

I go upstairs and put my ear flat against the heating register. I can hear every word.

Mama says, "Lucinda, she told me she was afraid she'd never have kids. Only had one ovary. And got a uterus half the normal size. Tilted, too."

"Poor thing," says Granny.

"And her being two hundred and fifty pounds," Mama goes on, "she was afraid she'd never have a husband, neither. Well, she up and meets this truck driver, Thornton Cuzick, and next thing you know, she's pregnant. Says to me, 'I'm a-keeping this baby, but I'm not a-marrying Thornton, that's for sure.'"

"Why not?" says Granny.

"Well, turns out, he's a kleptomaniac been arrested for stealing ladies' purses."

"My," says Granny.

"So she went back home to have her baby."

My ear's burning up against the grate, but I don't want to miss a word.

"Went back to Clarksville," Mama says.

"Indiana?" says Granny.

"Says her daddy works for the Clarksville Casket Company."

"Well."

"So Cuzick follows her down there and just won't give her no peace. Sets out in front of her house in a beat-up Cadillac when he ain't on the road. Follows her to work. Now she's snuck back here to visit her cousin. I seen her at the store today in her maternity dress." Mama scoots her chair. "Big as a house."

"Well," says Granny.

I can hear them clearing the table and pushing their chairs in.

I run to my room.

9.
Wonder Beans

Granny, she's a-setting in the living room with her medical encyclopedia. "I got me the rheumatiz," she says. "'Dull pain, can attack anywhere on the body. Often occurs before weather change.'"

"Must be going to rain," I say.

"Yep, must be." Granny looks up from her book again. "They got six different cures here. Two of them I've tried, and they ain't worked. Mary Mae, maybe you and me should walk on down to the pharmacy and see what we can turn up."

"Sure, Granny."

Granny gets on her knit hat she pulls down tight over her head, and we walk along, Granny tapping her cane on the sidewalk. She's got one made of birch, a real nice one that turns like a spiral.

✠ ✠ ✠

We stop off to see Little Lukey first, two doors down. That's Little Lukey Chassoldt, just one year old. He's beginning to walk, grabbing onto a chair and taking a few steps. He's got skin like suede, so soft you want to lick his cheek, only that ain't a good idea, since his mama don't want him getting sick. She thinks he's got a bad heart, and they got to be real careful.

I tell you what I love to see is my great-granny picking up Little Lukey and holding him close. They's eighty-some years apart and just the best of friends. Lukey, he'll try to pull her glasses off, and Granny says, "You like my glasses, don't you, Lukey, only you can't have them."

Granny bounces him a little. "I've held many a baby in my life," she says. "First there was your grandma and her three sisters. Then there was all their children, seven boys and eight girls, and then there was their children, Mary Mae and her cousins—how many now, Mary Mae? Is it thirty-three?"

"Yep, thirty-three with Cousin Wilmer."

Granny hands Little Lukey back to Mrs. Chassoldt.

"Lukey loves Granny," says Mrs. Chassoldt, waving Lukey's hand as we go.

⌗ ⌗ ⌗

Down at the pharmacy, they got a whole wall full of trial sizes, little packs of this and that, and Granny buys me some hand lotion, nail polish, and a box of gummy bears.

Granny gets a bottle of pills the druggist picks out, two jars of fruit juice, and a tub of muscle rub. Then we stop off at the grocery and pick up a sack of green beans.

"We'll make us some Wonder beans," she says. "Them's good for any ailment."

⌗ ⌗ ⌗

Me and Granny set down at the table, and she shows me how to do beans. You snap off the ends, peel the strings. Then she chops up some green onions. "You get the salt, vinegar, and thyme, Mary Mae."

Granny, she fries up some bacon, takes it out and puts the onions in the grease, cooks them a little, then adds hot water, the beans, and a little bit of salt, vinegar, and thyme.

Daddy comes home, says the place smells like a restaurant.

That night for dinner we have the Wonder beans with the crumpled-up bacon on top, along with Mama's pot roast. Then Granny goes into the hall and begins rubbing her back up against the wall. Making little hiccupping sounds or big, long belches. Bigger than Daddy's, even. I can't believe all that noise is coming out of my granny. "What are you doing, Granny?" I say.

"I'm releasing gas."

"Gas?"

"What I get when I eat Wonder beans. Doctor says I'm fortunate to be able to do this. Some people can't release it."

That's the thing about Granny. She has all sorts of habits. Like gargling salt water. Sniffing camphor. Blowing her nose like a lawn mower.

"It just ain't ladylike," Mama says to Daddy. "And her cussing," she says. "What gets into that woman?"

But I like all them habits.

✜ ✜ ✜

I'm up in Granny's room, and she's showing me more guitar chords.

"You're a natural, Mary Mae," says Granny. She puts her fiddle up to her chin, and we play together, like a little band. Sometimes she'll do fancy things, just a-rippling in over the top.

We make up another song together:

"Wonder beans, they're mighty fine.
Wonder beans, they're yours and mine.
Wonder beans, they're what I see.
Wonder beans, they're good for me.

"Take you a kettle, get you some bacon.
Fry her up, it's beans we're a-makin'.
Cook them beans in a little bit of water.
Add some salt the way you oughter.

"Wonder beans, they're mighty fine.
Wonder beans, they're yours and mine.
Wonder beans, they're what I see.
Wonder beans, they're good for me.

"Stand in the corner, feel that gas.
Rub your back and let her pass.
Burp yourself just like a baby.
Wonder Beans, I don't mean maybe."

Then we stop our music making and just tell stories.
"What kind of school did you go to when you was young, Granny?"

"I went to school up on Short Pine Creek. Had a man for a teacher. Bigger boys would sometimes give him a rough time. But he taught all of us, first grade to eighth. That's all the further I went. And you could get along, too, if that's all the further you went, but it's so nice to get an education," says Granny. "Me, I'd like to know what all them numbers mean in them scientific books."

Granny tells me more stories about how things used to be—making her first guitar out of rubber bands and a shoebox, traveling to towns with her sisters, singing on the radio—and then she collapses, says, "Oh my stomach, it's a-paining me." Or "Oh, my ar-thee-ri-tis, it's a-coming on strong." Or "Oh my rheu-ma-tiz." Or "Oh, my high blood."

Mama calls that being a hypochondriac, but I think maybe she really does feel bad, and when you get old, maybe all kinds of things fall apart.

10.
Heaven and Hell

Me, Chester, and Chloe finish coloring the Noah's Ark scene. Brother Lucas, Orlin, Jed, and Jonathan put our puppet theatre up on the stage in the church basement. Brother Lucas pulls the church curtains right up to the edge of the plywood, so we got the whole back stage to move around in.

Now we's all standing around with our puppets, except for Orlin who don't have no puppet since he's a-playing God.

I roll the black backdrop down for Day One, open up the curtains, and stand off to the side.

"Orlin, you start," says Brother Lucas.

Orlin, standing just behind the black cheesecloth, pulls his chin back way far and says, real serious, "Being the Supreme Being, I can see that the earth is without form and void." He pauses, holds up one arm. "Let there be light."

"You don't need no arm motions," says Jonathan Safer. "You're invisible."

"He's trying to feel the part," says Brother Lucas. "Quiet."

Jonathan's kneeling under the window in front of me. He shines his flashlight up onto the backdrop, and Jed Bean rattles a piece of sheet metal for thunder.

Orlin goes on in his Supreme Being voice. "That is good." But that don't sound important enough for Orlin, so he booms it out again. "I SAY THAT IS GOOD. VERY, VERY GOOD."

Jed Bean makes more thunder.

Orlin goes up to Day Five, booming out his "goods," me pulling down each backdrop. But them backdrops go clunk-clunk-clunk-clunk-clunk when the stick rolls over the plywood.

This makes an awful lot of noise. "Maybe we should fix that," I say.

"Don't fix it," says Orlin. "I like it. I like that noise."

I know why. He's thinking it sounds important, like God's got a big machine.

"Long as Orlin don't mind, I don't," says Brother Lucas. He runs through the rest of Creation, then has Eve and the Devil on Temptation, then Adam and Eve sneaking around in fig leaves. "Oops, we's out of time," says Brother Lucas. "We'll do Noah's Ark next Sunday."

"I want to do it today," I say. "I got a lot of questions."

"You'll just have to wait," says Brother Lucas.

✢ ✢ ✢

Granny and I sing "Just a Note from Jesus Christ," wrote by one of Granny's friends.

Sister Coates asks who would like to give thanks.

Chloe gets up. She holds her hands together like in prayer. "I'm grateful a little squirrel is living in my attic," she says. "Because I can hear him pitter-pat across the kitchen ceiling."

"Ain't that sweet," Mama whispers to me. I know she loves the way Chloe says "pitter-pat."

"I made the basketball team," says Jed Bean. He raises his fist and cheers, along with everybody else.

"Well, the Lord sure watched out for me this week," says Violet Ormsby. "Got me six free tickets to Show on Ice."

"Hallelujah! Praise the Lord."

✢ ✢ ✢

Sister Coates preaches on John 14:2. How the Lord has said, "In my father's house are many mansions. I go to prepare a place for you." She tells us what she thinks Heaven will be like. That God will have offices up there, and sometimes he'll have us doing errands for him. Be emissaries of the Lord, she says. Maybe spread his word to other planets.

Other planets, I'm thinking. Which ones? After service I ask Sister Coates.

"Mary Mae, I'm not exactly sure, but God can do whatever God puts his mind to."

"What kind of mind does God have?"

"Big. A trillion times bigger than yours and mine."

Hmm. Sounds like something I'm learning at school.

✠ ✠ ✠

Sunday night we're all a-setting in the living room, and I ask Daddy what *he* thinks Heaven will be like.

"There'll be lots of fishing," he says. "And a place to set and play cards."

But then Mama says, "No, it's going to be all hot fudge sundaes. And you won't get sick if you eat too many."

Granny says it's a place to sing up a storm. "They'll have the best instruments up there, probably always in tune."

So I think Heaven is what you want it to be.

"Does God have days and nights up there?" I ask Daddy.

"God has whatever God wants," Daddy says. "But I s'pect he's got mostly days."

"Will we have to sleep, or can we stay up all the time?"

"Probably whatever we please," he says. "Me, I'll take a little nap now and then."

So while we're all setting there together, I can't help but ask, "What's Hell like?"

"It ain't pretty," says Mama. "They's fires going all the time, and people that have been bad or ain't believed in the Lord Jesus, that's where they go."

"Do they ever get out?"

"Nope, they never get out. That's why you got to be careful." Now Mama's up and walking like Sister Coates. "You got to be ready for the Rapture, too, Mary Mae. Don't never step out of this house without thinking the Rapture might happen," she says. "You might be in an airplane, you might be riding an elevator, but when the time comes, the Lord will swoop you up. You want to be among the chosen, Mary Mae. You got to be ready, and you got to be good."

✠ ✠ ✠

But I ain't good, and sometimes I worry about it. Judgment Day will come, Mama's told me, and we will all be called to account for our actions. The high will be brought low. So I picture everyone marching along, stepping up to a big brown box with God setting behind it, like I seen on TV.

"Were you listening in when your mama was talking about the boarder?" God would ask.

"Yes, Lord," I'd say.

And God would say, "Did you dig up that trilobite?"

"Yes, Lord," I'd say. "But why did you leave all them little animals in the dirt if you didn't want us admiring them?"

I figure I've done lots of bad things in my life and have lots of marks under my name, and maybe God's keeping a tally, with all the bad things I done marked off in his book.

✛ ✛ ✛

"Granny, do you think the Lord keeps track of all the bad things we done?" I ask her before we go to bed.

"I s'pect he does," says Granny. "But I s'pect he's smiling when he sees the good things, too. Like when you get up and sing, I s'pect he's a-smiling big."

11.
Ranzone's Kitchen

Herschel's doing his report on starfish. Miss Sizemore gives him a book on them, and she finds me a book, too, *The Wonder of the Trilobite*. It shows trilobites found near the Falls of the Ohio. When the river's low, you can walk way out and see them, she says.

I'm learning all kinds of things from this book:

Trilobites had their stomachs in their heads.
They caught their food with their prickly legs.
Some trilobites carried their babies on their head
    in something called a bubble sac.
Lots of them had real good eyes, could see all the
    way around and behind.
When a trilobite molted, it broke the front of
    its shell, up near the head, and crawled out.

I put all that into my report and then turn it in.

At home me and Granny sing all the verses for our song.

"*Trilobite crab, trilobite crab,*
  He don't need no taxicab.
  Critter and a swimmer from another age.
  Don't need a tank and he don't need a cage.

"*Trilobite crab, trilobite crab,*
  Little bitty eyes and a nose like a scab.
  Rolls in a ball like a little pill bug.
  Swims in the water and he sings, 'Glub, glub.'

"*Trilobite crab, trilobite crab,*
  Who's his mom and who's his dad?
  Eats up worms, then rolls in a ball
  Hides from the squid with the big eyeball.

"*Trilobite crab, trilobite crab.*
  Rolls in the mud and likes to gab.
  Cracks his suit, that's how he grows.
  Molts his shell from head to toes."

Thursday, Granny says she'll take us all out to dinner. They got an early-bird special at Ranzone's Kitchen. That's Mama and Daddy's favorite restaurant.

There's a line out the door, but I don't mind since they got this big tank outside where you can watch the fish. It's like a playpen, and you can just stand there and look down on all them lobsters. They got a big old rubber band on each claw, I guess to keep them from tearing each other apart.

But there's this little crab a-setting in the corner all by hisself. If you ain't seen a crab, here's what one looks like. He's got a top like a mushroom, only it's hard, and all these little legs that come sprouting out like a spider's, and then under his chin, he's got these two little feelers he's a-rubbing together like he's trying to think of what to do next. But I tell you, that ain't nothing compared with his eyes—he's got eyes that look just like a trilobite's, setting on each side of his head.

This little crab, he's backed off and trying to stay away from them lobsters. You can tell he's scared, just shifting back and forth like a little prizefighter. And I get to thinking about my trilobite, him setting in the water five hundred million years ago, watching out for them squids that might eat him up.

And I know just by watching that crab that my trilobite was alive, whether Mama thinks so or not. I know the Lord loved that trilobite as much as he loves this crab.

Trilobite shells wasn't put in the ground to trick us. Them trilobites growed up and ate and swam and got scared just like the rest of us.

✚ ✚ ✚

The hostess says we're next, so I follow Mama, Daddy, and Granny into the dining room. Granny gets the shrimp scampi, Mama orders crab gumbo, and Daddy gets french-fried scallops. Me, I don't feel like eating what I've just been watching, so I order spaghetti.

Then Mama, Granny, and Daddy all set talking about Brother Lucas and how it's so nice he's doing a puppet show.

✚ ✚ ✚

November 3, it's Granny's eighty-seventh birthday. G-Maw, my real grandma, come—she looks just like Granny, only a little bit bigger—and Great-Uncle Jasper and my cousins from Bloodstone. We have hot dogs, and then give her a big old cake with tiers. Looks like a steamboat at Christmas. Granny opens up cards from her friends down in Crawdad.

I give her a cushion she can use for wooden seats. It's

blue corduroy with GRANNY wrote on it. Granny don't like them hard seats, has me get her a bed pillow all the time.

Mostly the cousins just give her little things—a tea sampler, some bubble bath, a book of old sayings, since they know she's a-going back to Crawdad and has to put everything in a suitcase.

We all go into the living room and sing. Give Granny a concert—me playing Granny's guitar. We sing some of her own songs and some just old-time tunes, like "Bonaparte's Retreat" and "Jenny Get Around" and "Wayfaring Stranger."

And then we's all taking pictures. Family shots with everyone crowded around. Granny and Mama, Daddy, and G-Maw taking turns doing the shooting.

✠ ✠ ✠

Day after Granny's birthday I'm in her room playing guitar again.

"Mary Mae, I got something I want to give you," she says. She pulls her box of music out from under the bed and asks me to pick it up. It's the one she always thumbs through when she's trying to figure out something to sing. All them scraps of paper and pieces of songs. "Some of these songs goes way back, and a lot of them ain't finished," she says. "You can do what you want with them. You're the one should have them."

"Granny, them's yours."

"No, I want to pass these on," she says. "I've had my fun. Now it's your turn. You're the one of all the cousins that cares about music, the one that's got the talent and desire."

"Thanks, Granny," I say.

"And I want you to keep my guitar, too."

"No, you got to have your guitar." I can't picture Granny without it.

"No," she says, "I'm a-taking my fiddle, and I got my Autoharp back home. That's enough. They need me to sing, I'll just play one of them."

So I pick up that guitar again and can't believe it's mine. Got little designs all across the top and a strap Granny made herself.

Then I look through the box of music. Some of them pages is real old—1937, 1942. All yellow and musty. Some got musical chords scribbled down. And some of them just got words. At the bottom of the box there's these old-time records. Big, heavy records.

"You'll have to get yourself a record player," says

Granny. "Watch for one at the Salvation Army that plays seventy-eights."

"Seventy-eights?" I say.

"Means the record goes around seventy-eight times per minute. That's how we got our sound in them days."

I got to ask Daddy can we get one of them players. I want to hear all Granny's records.

✧ ✧ ✧

Today at Sunday school me and Chester's supposed to practice. But Brother Lucas says Chester's home with the croup. "So I'm shortening Noah's Ark," he says. "That way Chester don't have much to learn."

"But then I won't have much to learn," I say.

"Nothing I can do about that," says Brother Lucas. "Here's how it's going to be. You and Noah's just tending ship. Them animals is already on the boat. The food's been picked up and stored. And it's been a-raining for three days."

"But we got us a backdrop with the animals marching in."

"Nope, they's already been marched in. We'll use the plain backdrop for you and Chester."

"But I want to know some things. How did Mrs. Noah collect all them pairs? And how did the tiger cats walk in all peaceful with the sheep and the goats? And who rounded up the Komodo dragons? And where did they get enough food? Some of them animals got to have fresh meat, lots of it."

"Can't answer them questions," says Brother Lucas. "We got a guest preacher speaking this morning."

"But I want to practice!" I say.

Even Chloe and Orlin think I should get some practice.

"Don't have time. Preacher's starting early, so we got to get upstairs."

✠ ✠ ✠

I think about skipping, hiding out in the bathroom and playing my guitar, but when I come up the stairs, I see this man up at the front of the church setting on a metal folding chair. He's got his foot twisted up by his mouth, and he's eating a doughnut off his big toe. Then I see that his sleeves is loose and empty and tucked into his pockets. The adult Bible class is already in their seats. After our class sets down, Sister Coates introduces him. "Pastor Hosea Tilbury," she says. "We are pleased to have him here from Morning, Oklahoma."

His wife is a-setting off to the side.

"He's wrote six books," Sister Coates says, "just typing with his toes." We can see them all lined up on the offering table. Sister Coates reads their titles. *Swinging with the Lord, Talking with the Lord, First Supper, Last Supper, God's Fat Calf,* and the one that was a Christian bestseller, *Pearls of Oklahoma.*

Pastor Tilbury stands. "I was born this way," he says. "But my mama and daddy saw to it that I rose to the challenge." He sets back down, shows us how he can do different things, like tie his shoe with his teeth, write his name with his toes, or comb his hair. He's got on socks that fit like gloves, each toe separate.

During question time, Jonathan Safer wants to know if Pastor Tilbury can work a puppet.

"Show me one," he says, and Jonathan hands him Adam. He takes it in his teeth by the hair, sticks his foot up the body, then turns his own self upside down quick as a doorknob. Now the puppet is straight up in the air and Pastor Tilbury's a-looking at us upside down and talking. "Don't let the Devil take your courage," he says.

We all applaud. He flips the puppet off, catches it in his teeth, then turns hisself right-side up.

✠ ✠ ✠

Granny and I sing "Wings of Jesus, Let Me Soar," a tune she found in an old hymnbook.

Sister Coates asks who would like to give thanks.

"I'm grateful the Lord brung Pastor Tilbury to our church," says Rowena Chisholm.

"And we know how courageous we can be," says Ruth Truesdell.

"Praise the Lord," says Sister Coates.

She leaves her microphone fastened to the podium. Pastor Tilbury digs into his briefcase with his toes, puts his sermon in his mouth, stands, walks to the podium, puts the sermon down, and turns up the first page with his tongue. "Hallelujah, we are blessed!" he says.

"Amen!" says Mama, though I don't listen to a word after that. I'm still fussing I didn't get no puppet show practice.

12.
Ice Age

Monday, Miss Sizemore gives us back our reports. Me and Herschel got A's. Then she gives back all the fossils that was on the display table. I get my little trilobite, and them other fossils I dug up with the class, wrap them up in my old sock, and put them in my book bag.

Miss Sizemore's taken down all the pictures from the Ordovician age and put up new posters showing how the Ohio River valley looked during the ice age—with woolly mammoths and mastodons, peccaries and musk-oxen, saber-toothed tigers and giant sloths, and a lot of other animals I write down. She hands out maps on glaciers, showing how three of them come down over Ohio. "The last one, the Wisconsonian, left piles of gravel," she says.

After recess, she leads our class down Mason Street, then straight up through the woods, till we're standing at the edge of the grassy part overlooking the city. Miss

Sizemore's wearing sneakers and a jacket, and the wind's blowing her red hair all around in the sun like a dandelion. She points down to Hanrahan Street, at the foot of the hill, says that's where the Ohio River used to flow, looping around toward the expressway.

"You mean the Ohio River used to come through DeSailles?" says Dexter Bodley.

"Fifty thousand years ago," says Miss Sizemore. "But the glaciers pushed it south, and when the last one melted, it left a pile of gravel." I'd seen that gravel lots of times, but never knowed it was left by a glacier. We all look down to the foot of the cliff, and there it is. "That gravel is called a glacial moraine," says Miss Sizemore. Me and Herschel pick up a few pieces on the way back.

Then Miss Sizemore leads our class down Hanrahan Street, the old bed of the river.

Even Shirley Whirly's spooked. "We'd be thirty feet under," she says.

Just thinking about the ice age gives me the shivers. All them animals wandering around, and the glacier moving and creaking. I start thinking about them icy-blue Popsicles they got down at the pony keg, the ones that stick to your tongue, and how the world must have been that color then.

And I'm thinking if the Lord wanted to do us in again, he could turn the whole world into an ice ball.

✛ ✛ ✛

I show Granny the glacier maps and tell her about walking down the bed of the old river.

"Lordy," she says, "musta been cold."

"They was lots of animals living around here, too," I say. "Saber-toothed tigers and big giant sloths and peccaries." I show her my list.

"What's a peccary?" says Granny.

"Like a pig. Got a big, long snout."

I go upstairs, pull my cigar box out, and add the fossils and gravel to my collection, then come back down.

Granny gets her fiddle, I get my guitar, and we make up a song.

"Peccary a-nosing down the glacier in the morning,
  Yellow-bellied sapsucker finds him a tree.
  Woodchuck says, 'I'm a-looking for some huckleberries.'
  Short-faced bear says, 'Come with me.'"

We sing that verse again, trying to ease into a second verse. We's trying different chords, different words. Then

Mama comes home. She sets her things down in the kitchen, goes upstairs. Me and Granny's quiet for a few seconds, thinking. And then I hear Mama. Throwing things around. Mumbling real loud. Next thing I know, Mama's clomping down the stairs.

She's got my cigar box.

I forgot to hide it.

"Mary Mae," she says, "I thought I told you to throw these out." She slams the box down on the coffee table. I picture the trilobite banging heads with the crinoid.

Then she picks up my "Interview with a Trilobite." I showed Granny but forgot to put it away. "I told you, you was not to study such things. You was to tell your teacher to give you other assignments."

I glance at Granny.

She's putting her fiddle away, but I know she's taking it all in.

"So what I got to do," says Mama, "and I don't want to do it—Lord knows I got enough to do at work—but as a Christian person, I got to take you out of school."

"We're building a glacier tomorrow."

"You ain't a-building nothing. This is where you're having school from now on. You ain't a-playing music, neither." She takes my guitar, puts it in the closet. Then she picks up my cigar box and takes it out to the trash.

✛ ✛ ✛

Daddy comes home.

"We got a problem," says Mama. "I'm telling you, Farley, I can't have this. Mary Mae's writing papers on things we don't believe in."

"Like what?" says Daddy. He don't know what she's talking about.

"Trailerbites."

"*Trilo*bites," I say.

"I don't care what they's called," says Mama. "Them's trick rocks. Belong in the ground, and you didn't throw them out when you was told to."

Daddy still don't know what she's talking about, but he chimes in, "Should have listened to your mama."

"I got no choice, Farley."

Daddy's raising his eyebrows, like as if to ask what.

"Got to teach her at home," says Mama.

"Is that allowed?" says Daddy.

"You bet it is," she says. "I been reading about it in *Christian Testament*."

"But how are you going to do that and work?"

"We'll just get up early," says Mama. "I'll give Mary Mae her assignments, and Granny can make sure she does them. You don't mind, do you, Granny?"

"I'm here all day," says Granny. "Though I ain't going to be here forever."

"We'll worry about that when the time comes," says Mama.

"You got to know what you're doing," Daddy says to Mama.

"Farley, I can teach," says Mama. "You just make assignments. Besides," she says, going to the sink for water, "I been to college."

Mama's got a business certificate.

"We get Mary Mae on the right track," says Mama, "we can let her go to public high school."

"High school! I'll run away before I have to wait for high school," I say.

Mama slaps my face. "I don't care what you want. We're going down to school tomorrow, picking up your things, then coming back home." Mama sets back down.

"I ain't eating dinner," I say, and I go upstairs. I go into my room and set on my bed. Then I see Mrs. Noah, perched on that pop bottle on my dressing table. Now, I love Mrs. Noah—especially since I done her face myself—but I hate Mama right now more than I love Mrs. Noah, so I grab her by the hair and take her downstairs. Mama, Daddy, and Granny's still setting in the kitchen. I walk past, waving that puppet, go out the back door to the garbage can. I throw Mrs. Noah on top of my cigar box. Then I come back in. "I ain't a-playing Mrs. Noah, neither," I say.

"Yes you are, young lady," says Mama. "You go out and take that puppet out of the trash!"

"No, just leave it there," says Daddy. "She'll have no privileges for a month."

"I ain't got no privileges now," I say, and stomp back upstairs.

"I want her in that puppet play," I hear Mama saying.

"Then you better save that puppet," says Daddy.

"Well, Farley, you're closer to the door."

I'm pleased to hear them arguing over Mrs. Noah. I plop down by the register. I can hear Mama on the phone telling Mr. Harbin she'll be late tomorrow. And then she calls Sister Coates. "Sister Coates is a-praying for us," she says.

Daddy calls me for dinner.

"I ain't coming down," I say.

"You're coming down here," says Mama, yelling up the stairs.

"You're coming down right now," says Daddy.

So I come down, but I don't eat nothing. Just push my food around.

"Eat!" says Mama. Then she shakes her head. "What did I do to deserve this?"

I clear the table, then go back up to my room.

⊹ ⊹ ⊹

I hear Granny when she comes up to her room, and I go stand in her doorway. "It ain't fair, Granny," I tell her.

"No, it ain't," she says. "What you gonna do about it?"

"I'm running away," I say.

"Where to?"

"Zimbabwe."

"What would you do there?" says Granny.

"I don't know. Pick fruit."

"Well I'd think twice about that."

"You ain't no help," I say.

I go to my room, climb into bed with my clothes on. I ain't never going to sleep.

⊹ ⊹ ⊹

But I wake up at midnight. House is quiet. I creep downstairs, open up the back door, and walk out to the trash. With the moon, it's light enough to see. I lift up a garbage bag, and there's my cigar box. Mrs. Noah's missing. I feel around in some potato peels, find two fossils that fell out, and put them back in the box. I take it out, put the garbage back in, put the lid back on.

Then I look up at the stars. Miss Sizemore says each

one of them stars is the center of a universe just like ours. It makes my head swoosh just thinking about it and how compared to the world, I'm no bigger than a dust mite. Except unless God thinks I'm important. I hope he thinks I'm important. Lord help me, I say. I want to stay in Miss Sizemore's class. She's the best teacher I've ever had.

13.
Mr. Trimble's

I don't feel like brushing my teeth or washing my face, so I don't. And I have on what I slept in, but Mama don't even notice. She plaits my hair, yanking it hard. We get into the car. I don't think I should have to go to school if I can't stay there. Mama could turn my books in for me and pick up my school supplies.

She puts on her best slacks, the ones with the cuffs, and we drive down to school. She parks out in front of the new addition, and we walk up to Mr. Trimble's office. He's the principal.

Mama stiffens up the minute she walks into his office. It's filled with sculptures he's built out of Popsicle sticks—a castle, a Ferris wheel, a fort, and dangling over the copy machine, something that looks like a space station.

"Good morning, Mary Mae," he says. "And Mrs. Krebs?"

Him and Mama shake hands.

"What can I do for you?"

Mama clears her throat. "Mary Mae ain't a-going to school no more."

"Oh?" Mr. Trimble straightens his glasses. "Are you moving?"

"No, we ain't a-moving," says Mama. "I'm teaching Mary Mae at home."

"I see." Mr. Trimble looks sort of mixed up. "Why don't you have a seat?" Me and Mama set down on folding chairs, and Mr. Trimble calls Miss Sizemore up on the intercom. "Please come down," he says. "We have Mary Mae and her mother here."

He arranges some papers on his desk, pins an announcement to his bulletin board, then takes a note from a first-grader.

He sets down, and in comes Miss Sizemore.

"Morning, Mary Mae," she says. "And you must be Mrs. Krebs." She puts out her hand and Mama shakes it, though I know she don't want to. Miss Sizemore pulls up a chair.

"Mrs. Krebs says she's taking Mary Mae out of school," Mr. Trimble tells Miss Sizemore. "She wants to teach her at home." Then he says to Mama, "Can you tell us why?"

Mama tells them about the fossils and the paper I

oughtn't to have written. "We don't believe in trilobites," she says, showing him my interview.

I'm a-staring off at the ceiling, my hands going hot and cold at the same time.

"We believe the world is six thousand years old," says Mama, "and as a Christian person, I can't have Mary Mae learning otherwise."

"I'm sorry," says Miss Sizemore. "I try to present the latest research, and I like the children to discover things themselves. I would love to keep Mary Mae in class—she's an inspiration. Why don't I modify her assignments?"

"No, I already told Mary Mae to ask for different assignments, and she didn't. I think you provide too much temptation. So I got to take Mary Mae out of school to make sure she learns the right things. I got to keep my own conscience clear."

"Mama, I want to stay in school," I say.

But Mama won't hear of it. "Mary Mae, give Miss Sizemore your books."

"She's welcome to keep her books," says Mr. Trimble. "She can have them on loan."

"No," says Mama, "I don't trust them books."

So I'm busy digging through my backpack, pulling out my books and putting them on Mr. Trimble's desk. I'm

so embarrassed, tears are coming up in my eyes. And now a
hot flood spills out over my cheeks.

Mr. Trimble and Miss Sizemore just set quiet, and then
all of a sudden Mr. Trimble says to Mama, "Do you have a
copy of your curriculum?"

"Curriculum?" says Mama.

"Your course of study," says Mr. Trimble. "We'll all be
in trouble unless I have your curriculum. The school board
will require it."

"Oh yes, what I'm teaching," says Mama. "Well as far
as I'm concerned, the Bible's the only book she'll need!"

"Children need to be well rounded," says Miss Sizemore.
"They need history and science. And art—art is important."

"Mary Mae gets her art at Sunday school," says Mama.
"As for history and science—they's right in the Bible."

"But we need to know your curriculum," says Mr.
Trimble. "What you're studying in the Bible. What lessons
you're teaching."

Mama's pinned down here and don't know which way
to go. "Hmmmph," she says. "Well, I can bring it in next
Monday."

"Monday will be fine," says Mr. Trimble.

You can tell Mama didn't know she'd be asked for
that. She picks up her pocketbook. "Miss Sizemore, if it's
all right, Mary Mae will go up and clear out her desk."

I walk up to the classroom with Miss Sizemore.

"I'm sorry," says Miss Sizemore. "I wish I'd known. You know, I could have given you different assignments, the way I do Shirley Whirly."

"Nope," I say. "I like science. I want what everybody else gets." Then I get a lump so big in my throat I can't even talk. I stop in the hall outside my class and wipe my face. Don't want nobody in the class to know I been crying.

Then I go in and fill my backpack up with school supplies.

"What's going on?" says Herschel, soon as I'm pulling my things out of my desk.

"Mama's taking me out of school," I say. I don't tell him no more. He can figure it out.

"Wish my mama'd take *me* out of school," says Shirley Whirly.

✛ ✛ ✛

I go out to my locker, get my gym clothes and art supplies, then go back downstairs.

Mama's standing outside Mr. Trimble's office.

14.
Mama's Curriculum

I swear, that principal," says Mama, walking into the house. Granny's setting at the kitchen table. "I don't know how he runs that school—got a whole office full of Tinkertoys."

"Them ain't Tinkertoys," I say. "Them's Popsicle sticks, and he builds things for a hobby."

"Hobbies don't belong in school," says Mama. She starts going through drawers to find school supplies—pencils, scrap paper, pens from Harbin Plumbing.

"Let's see what you have in that school bag," she says.

I pour everything out, including a compass and a protracter.

"We'll just work here at the kitchen table," says Mama. "Don't need no fancy desk. Get your Bible."

I go up to my room and bring it down.

She sets down and starts thumbing through hers.

"All right, Mary Mae, I want you to read Matthew 13, all them parables. And after that"—she's looking through her Bible again—"you can study for a spelling test. Thirteen books of the Bible. First column. I'll give you a test as soon as I come home."

Mama puts her coat back on. "Granny, you and Mary Mae can have them cold cuts for lunch. And Mary Mae"—she comes over, puts her hand on my shoulder—"you're my own precious daughter, and I'm doing this for your own good."

She kisses my forehead.

I wipe it off.

Mama runs out the door.

✠ ✠ ✠

I just set at the table for a time, don't even speak to Granny. And Granny putters around like everything's normal. I got a good mind not to do nothing—not to read, not to learn my spelling. What's Mama going to do, take me to the principal?

Granny sets down and opens up her Bible. I see she's looking at Matthew 13. "I like parables," she says. "They's all nice little stories."

"I don't care," I say. "I ain't reading 'em."

"Might as well read until you figure out what to do."

"Ain't nothing I *can* do." I start to cry.

"You'll figure something out," says Granny. "You got a curiosity like I do, got to learn everything you can. Meantimes, I'd keep your mama happy by reading them parables."

I draw circles with my compass. Then I draw circles inside circles. Then circles that go right off the page. Finally I get my Bible and start looking at them parables. I read real slow. "Granny," I say, "I got questions."

"Shows you're thinking," says Granny. "Write them down and save them for your mama."

So I write them down.

Verses I Got Questions About

1—What seaside was Jesus setting at?

7—How can thorns choke seeds?

12—Why does the Lord say that for him that has more, he'll get more, and for him that don't have much, he'll get even less. That don't seem fair.

15—What does "waxed gross" mean?

21—Why does Matthew always call them people "the multitude"?

47—How is the kingdom of Heaven like a net?
56—Who was Jesus' sisters?

Then I study my spelling words. Only hard one's Deuteronomy. And I really only got eleven names to learn, since there's Samuel I and II and Kings I and II.

I've done finished with everything by noon. Granny and I have our cold cuts, me eating half the package.

Granny wants to know do I want to do some singing. "No," I say. Singing might cheer me up.

So I just read my Bible, then go looking for Mrs. Noah. She ain't nowhere in the kitchen, and she ain't in none of Mama's drawers.

✛ ✛ ✛

Mama comes home from work. "How'd everything go?" she says.

I hand her my list. "I got some questions," I say.

"Right now I want you to help me carry some things in. They had a set of encyclopedias down at the shop, and Mr. Harbin said we could have them."

I bring them in, put them on the dining-room table. It's the Finley & Watson *Whole World Encyclopedia* in twenty volumes. They smell like rags. First thing I do is look up *tri-lobite*. They got it, but it's only one paragraph. And there ain't no pictures.

✣ ✣ ✣

Then Wanda Brierly from church stops off at six o'clock with a fifth grade math book. "I used this with my son when he broke his leg," she says. "Course, that was a long time ago."

The kid on the cover's playing with a Hula Hoop.

I hear Wanda say to Mama, "Well, it's better she be here than back at school digging up them fossils."

Soon as she's gone, I read one of the story problems out loud.

> "Virginia is having a birthday party. She has fifteen guests and would like to buy everyone a nickel candy bar. In addition, she would like to have paper hats that cost eight cents a piece and a cake that costs $2.95. Nut cups are four cents a piece, and a large jar of nuts is ninety-nine cents. How much money will Virginia need?

"Mama, I can't use this book. It says candy bars is a nickel."

"Don't matter," says Mama. "Numbers is numbers."

"And nobody wears paper hats no more, neither."

"We'll just have to make do," says Mama.

"When are we doing my spelling test?" I say.

"After dinner," says Mama.

I don't eat much. Want everyone to be reminded I ain't pleased.

⊹ ⊹ ⊹

After dinner Mama gives me my spelling test. "The ones at school we had was much harder," I tell her. I show Mama my list of questions again on Matthew 13.

"Did you show them to Granny?" she says.

"Granny says to show them to you."

Mama sighs, takes a look. "Use the encyclopedia," she says. "That's what I got it for."

"But what should I look up?"

"Parables!"

So I look it up, but it's only got one paragraph, says parables was told by Jesus.

"Mama, the encyclopedia ain't no help. You got to explain things, Mama. Miss Sizemore explains things, and she has discussions."

Mama thumps the table. "I'm getting tired of you talking about Miss Sizemore. She may explain things and have discussion, but she ain't a-telling you God's truth. Let me see them questions."

I hand them to her.

"First of all," says Mama, "it don't matter what sea Jesus was at. Why do you want to know?"

"I just do. So I can look it up on the map."

"You don't need to look it up on the map. It ain't important." Mama takes a deep breath. "I'm sorry, Mary Mae. You do need them questions answered. But I can't do it right now. Soon's I get my curriculum done, I'll answer your questions."

"You can't answer no questions because you don't know how to teach!" I tell her. "And I'm tired of your stupid lessons."

"You don't talk to your mama that way," she says.

Even Granny gives me a look.

✢ ✢ ✢

Mornings, Mama gives me a bunch of problems in that math book and something to read in the Bible. She's jumping all over the place. "Why are we going from parables to Psalms, Mama?" I say.

"Don't ask questions," she says. "Just read." Then she adds, "I'm doing the best I can, Mary Mae."

At night Mama sets down at the dining-room table with her Bible and tries making notes on her curriculum.

"What's a curriculum, anyway?" I hear her muttering. She gets the dictionary. "'Curriculum,'" she reads aloud, "'course of study.'" Mama sighs. "That's what I'm a-trying for. This weekend I'll figure it out."

✠ ✠ ✠

Herschel Cadwallader calls, and Mama puts me on. He's never called me before. He says he carved a woolly mammoth today out of Ivory soap. "Wish you was in school," he says. "I got me some new fossils for my collection."

"What kind?"

"Found me some crinoids down at Duck Creek. Me and Dexter walked down there. It was fun. When you coming back?"

I swallow hard. "I don't know. Never."

✠ ✠ ✠

Saturday, Mama makes more notes. I hear her talking to Sister Coates. "I thought teachers just made assignments—give a little spelling, a little history, a little math. But it ain't that easy." She hangs up and cries.

I look out the window and pray.

✛ ✛ ✛

Lord, I'm happy my mama's crying. And I'm real sorry I'm happy. It ain't Christian. But you got to do something. Reading your Bible's nice, but we're jumping all over the place. And I can't take no more of this moldy encyclopedia, and I don't like this math book.

✛ ✛ ✛

Saturday evening we's eating dinner and the doorbell rings. It's our old boarder, Lucinda. She's in a rainbow-striped poncho and yellow tennis shoes, and wants to know can she stay overnight.

"My cousin's dropped me off," she says. "I can't stay there no more. They been evicted." She starts to cry.

Lot of folks been crying lately. Me. Mama. Lucinda.

"Honey, you can sleep on the couch," says Mama. She always did like Lucinda. Said she was the most innocent-est person she'd ever met in her life. Just didn't know how to take care of herself.

"And I have a favor," says Lucinda. She's sniffling more, choking down big sobs. "Can you take me to the bus station tomorrow morning? I know it's Sunday, but it's Daddy's birthday tomorrow and I told him I'd be home."

Lucinda's looking real tired, her being pregnant, and her hat's on crooked, with the tassel swinging down in her face.

"I don't think you should be riding a bus down there, you being eight months pregnant," says Mama. She glances at Granny. "Why don't me and Granny take you down to Clarksville?"

Granny nods.

"Oh I couldn't ask that," says Lucinda.

"No, we want to," says Mama. She goes over and closes her Bible. "That school can wait one more week for their curriculum."

Funny how Mama can do that. Now if I was to go to Miss Sizemore and say, "You can wait one more week for my report," I'd be in trouble. Would get my paper marked down for being late—and for being a smart aleck besides.

"Church can do without us for one Sunday, too," says Mama.

Church, I'm thinking. I'd like to skip church since Brother Lucas won't let me practice. And going down to Clarksville would get me out of here. Besides, Lucinda's my friend, too. We used to play Chutes and Ladders. "I want to go, too," I say. I smile and try to make up for my meanness.

"No, you and Daddy's going to church," says Mama.

"I gotta work," says Daddy.

"Sunday?"

"We got two trucks coming in for emergency service."

Mama shakes her head. I know she's fed up with me, plus she don't want me in the car when they're discussing Lucinda's condition.

So when Lucinda wanders off to the bathroom, I whisper to Mama, "I know all about Lucinda. She's pregnant and ain't married to her boyfriend."

Mama rolls her eyes. "You got puppet show practice."

I want to say I ain't got no puppet, but then she'll be reminded of my throwing Mrs. Noah into the trash. Besides, I know she's hid off in one of Mama's drawers. "I'm ready for the puppet show," I say. "We've done had all the practices we need. And Brother Lucas won't answer none of my questions."

"That's because you ask too many," says Mama.

✠ ✠ ✠

Mama calls Sister Coates to tell her we won't be in church tomorrow. Later I hear Mama telling Granny, "Sister Coates says it's so nice we're helping Lucinda. Says Wilma Tatters can play piano."

15.
Falls of the Ohio

Lucinda drags her duffle bag into the kitchen and shows us how she keeps her underwear in plastic food bags. "That way I can keep things nice and neat," she says.

Her and Mama make pancakes.

We leave the house about eight o'clock and take I-71 South. I want to say to Mama it's too bad we don't have no more of them John 3:16 stickers. But I'm still being punished, and I don't want to overdo my niceness.

We drive through Kentucky listening to *Vernon Valley Gospel Hour*.

And then Mama asks Lucinda if she's heard from Thornton.

"Not for a while," she says. "He might be locked up."

I see Mama glancing through the rearview mirror at me. She don't like me hearing such things.

"He comes around you again," says Granny, "you just get the law."

"I will," says Lucinda.

We drive past Carrollton, then cross the river at Louisville into Indiana. Lucinda's giving directions.

⊹ ⊹ ⊹

She lives on Whippet Street, near the Ohio River. We drive down this road under a big railroad trestle, and off in the distance there's a dam. We pass a sign that says FALLS OF THE OHIO. I'm wondering where I've seen that at. Falls of the Ohio. Then I remember—that was in the book Miss Sizemore give me, *The Wonder of the Trilobite*. It's where some of them fossils was dug up.

"Lots of driftwood down there," says Lucinda. "When the river's low, there's heaps of it along the bank."

"I'd like some of that," says Mama.

"Pull over," says Lucinda. "We got time."

Mama parks, and we walk down the stairs. "Now be careful," says Mama. It's a long ways down. Mama's helping Granny, who's holding on to the banister, and Lucinda's taking it slow, too. I lead the way, kicking seedpods off the stairs.

I can see the riverbed out there, like I seen in Miss Sizemore's book, and the little pools of water, and when I get down off the stairs, I start seeing fossils. Everywhere fossils. Like God come down and pressed fossils into the riverbed.

The sky's overcast now, so you don't have to squint.

Mama settles Granny down on the bottom step. "You just set right down here," says Mama.

"You all go on out there," says Granny. "I'll be all right."

"Over here's the best driftwood," says Lucinda. She points off to the left, where it's heaped against the bank, left from the last time the river rose.

But Mama don't even look at that driftwood. She's picking her way across the riverbed. Me and Lucinda's right behind.

"Look at this, Mary Mae," says Mama. "You can see these little plants left in the mud."

"That ain't mud," says Lucinda. "That's limestone."

"Can't be," says Mama. "A river's got mud." Mama probably thinks them plants is from last summer.

"Not here," says Lucinda. She gets down on her hands and knees in her rainbow poncho. "These little fossils here is millions and millions of years old. My grade school brung us down, told us all about it. And us kids used to play here. We'd take little pieces home. Course you ain't allowed to do that no more."

It's funny that Mama don't argue with Lucinda. Mama's on her knees now, just running her fingers over them patterns.

"Sometimes if you wet something, you can see it better," says Lucinda. She splashes water from a little pool up onto a sponge fossil. "Ain't that beautiful!"

"Oh yes," says Mama, "and what's this?" She's pointing to something at the edge of a crevice.

I take a look. "It's a trilobite," I say.

"Looks like a crab," says Mama.

"Yep, they's related." I don't say nothing about how old it is. Lucinda already done that. "And here's a crinoid." I point out the tassel. "And over here's sponges, and look at this, it's a pipe organ coral." I never seen that except in the book Miss Sizemore give me. Wish I could tell her.

Mama's taken with this place. It's all here, millions of fossils, like the Lord's science lesson.

"This all used to be ocean," says Lucinda, standing up.

Mama don't argue. She's just running her fingers over them fossils.

I'm picturing how it was, millions of years ago, with the warm salt water, and palm fronds and jellyfish and trilobites and squids.

But it's beginning to rain.

We pick our way across the rocks to the steps where Granny sets.

"River ain't usually this low," says Lucinda. "We need this."

We all pile into the car and drop Lucinda off on Whippet Street. Her daddy's setting on the porch waiting for her.

✛ ✛ ✛

Granny dozes off on the way home, and Mama don't say a word. I'm thinking I better say something now before Mama forgets what she seen. "Them fossils was really interesting, wasn't they?" I say.

But Mama don't answer.

"It was like a science lesson, wasn't it, Mama?"

She still don't answer.

"Be nice if we could go there again, wouldn't it? And take our time and look at everything."

Mama's still quiet. Then she says, "Mary Mae, it's something we shouldn't be looking at."

"The riverbed?"

"Them fossils," she says. "They's not meant for us to see, Mary Mae."

"But they's out there," I say.

✛ ✛ ✛

We get lunch at the Dog-Gone-It Café in Sparta. Old people dressed in church clothes is a-coming in.

"I missed going to church this morning," says Mama.

"Me, too," says Granny.

"I missed singing," I say. "But I liked seeing that river-bed."

"Mary Mae, I don't want to hear nothing more about that riverbed."

"It's God's creation, Mama. No sense in not talking about it."

"I told you I've heard enough."

✛ ✛ ✛

Mama orders us all the Sunday special—fried chicken with mashed potatoes and gravy—but I'm back to not eating again.

✛ ✛ ✛

We get home at three, and Mama opens up her Bible and starts working on her curriculum. I go upstairs and dig my cigar box out of my dressing table. I pull all them fossils out and line them up. Then I wait for them to talk to me.

"Wish you could put us out on a shelf, Mary Mae," they say. "Sure would be nice."

"I'll do my best," I say. I pack them all up again, hide them away, and go downstairs.

✠ ✠ ✠

Ain't allowed to go out in the neighborhood, but I can still go out in my own backyard. It's quit raining, and I'm a-walking around in the wet. Sneakers getting all shushy. I go climb on the fishpond. Daddy keeps saying he's going to tear it down, but he don't. When we moved in, I was never allowed to climb on it or nothing because a kid could get hurt there, Daddy said. But I'm ten years old now. It's a whole lot of rocks all piled up, and there's a cement basin for water, only we ain't never filled it. Anyways, I climb up on it. I squat down and I'm a-looking around, and then I just about slide off into the basin. Can't believe what I'm seeing. Every slab of rock is teeming with fossils. Just like them slabs down at school.

Must have been dug up from the ground here.

Slabs so thick with fossils it looks like crab gumbo.

Fossils even thicker than they was at Falls of the Ohio. Or at school. I'm climbing all over them rocks like a chipmunk. In one slab there's six little trilobites enrolled together.

I go into the garage and get three lawn chairs. Line them up in front of the fishpond.

When Daddy comes home, I invite everyone out to see.

"I'm busy," says Mama.

"I'm tired," says Daddy.

"No, you got to see this."

"I'll go," says Granny. So Mama and Daddy follow her out.

"Take your seats," I say. "I got something to talk about."

Mama says, "Do this fast. It's cold out here."

"Now you see this here fishpond," I say. "Daddy, where do you think these rocks come from?"

"I s'pect right here in this yard," he says. "You go deep enough, you'll hit bedrock."

"Do you agree, Mama?" I say.

"I guess. But I think they'd have been smarter to use them rocks for steppingstones."

"Granny, what kind of rocks are these? It's something I told you."

"I do believe they's limestone," says Granny.

"Limestone," I say. "That's right. And shale. And what do you know, they's just a-teeming with fossils."

"Fossils?" says Daddy.

"Trilobites and brachiopods and crinoids and snails and sponges and starfish."

"Where?" says Mama.

"Come over here," I say, and I point them all out.

"Where did you learn about this?" says Daddy. He's climbing up top of the fishpond.

"School."

Daddy looks at Mama. "What are we keeping her home for?"

"She oughtn't to be learning such things," says Mama.

"But this is our backyard," says Daddy. "Can't go walking around like an ostrich."

"Them fossils was put in the ground to trick us, Farley," says Mama.

"Trick us?" says Daddy. "Who's trying to trick us?"

"The Lord," says Mama.

"If that's what the Lord's up to, you can go to church yourself. I ain't a-going."

Daddy takes off for the house. Mama runs after him.

I follow them in, try to listen, but they's in their room with the door shut.

⊹ ⊹ ⊹

At dinner, when the hamburger casserole comes around, I just out and say it: "I want to go to school tomorrow."

"You ain't a-going nowhere," says Mama. "I won't have no more talk about school or fossils."

"Lavernia, you're being stubborn," says Daddy.

"Maybe I am, but I got to do what's right," says Mama.

"It ain't right keeping me from learning things," I say.

"Enough!" says Mama.

"You're so worried about what's not in the Bible," says Daddy. "Lot of things ain't in the Bible. Cars and trucks ain't in the Bible. But I believe in 'em. Ain't no reason not to."

But Mama's the one that brung Daddy to the Lord, so she's the expert. Mama pushes off from the table. "I'm a-calling Sister Coates," she says.

I clear the table, then stick around, hoping to listen, but as soon as Mama picks up the phone, she says, "Mary Mae, get upstairs."

So I go set by the register.

I hear Mama explaining to Sister Coates all about fossils and curriculum, and then I don't hear nothing. Mama's listening. And then I hear, "But I've had some college. And I used to teach Sunday school."

16.
Noah's Ark

Monday morning Mama's at the table finishing her grape-fruit and Mrs. Noah's setting on the kitchen table. Her hair's all flat on one side from being hid away. I pick her up, fluff her out. Granny's at the kitchen sink.

"Today you better get back to Genesis," says Mama. "Review for the puppet show."

"I ain't doing no puppet show," I say. I drop Mrs. Noah back down on the table.

"You'll do it," says Mama. "Whole church is depending on you. Now you get your Bible out and review. Granny, you're in charge."

✠ ✠ ✠

"I got a good mind to put Mrs. Noah back in the trash," I say to Granny after Mama leaves for work.

"I wouldn't do that," says Granny.

"Why not?"

"She might have something to say."

"Like what?"

"You're the one should be telling me."

I grab Mrs. Noah by the hair, take her upstairs, and put her on that pop bottle. Then I put all my fossils in a circle around her.

"I seen Noah's ark when it come floating over," says the trilobite.

"Me, too," says the crinoid.

"And I heard Mrs. Noah just a-yelling her head off," says the spiny coral.

"Is that true?" I say to Mrs. Noah.

"Lord, yes," says Mrs. Noah. "I like to died on that ship."

✠ ✠ ✠

I pull Mrs. Noah off the pop bottle and go back downstairs. "You know what, Granny, I don't think Mrs. Noah liked tending them animals."

Granny takes a sip of coffee. "Why not?"

I put Mrs. Noah on my hand, work her arms a little.

Then I take her off and look up Noah's ark in the encyclopedia. I'm expecting a little bitty paragraph, but it's a whole big article. Three pages. Talks about the problems a boat like that would have had.

So I'm reading and writing and thinking. I still don't have answers to a lot of my questions, but it's give me ideas for things I can have Mrs. Noah say.

⊹ ⊹ ⊹

Me and Granny have lunch, then Granny wants to go out back to the fishpond. She's wrapped in a shawl, setting in her lawn chair, and I'm a-climbing over the rocks.

"Now tell me more about them fossils," says Granny.

"They's older than the dinosaurs," I tell her. "And they lived in the sea." I point out all kinds of brachiopods and some horned corals. "Miss Sizemore says the world is fifteen billion years old, and these here critters come along in the Ordovician period. That's five hundred million years ago."

Granny's clicking her teeth. "Hmm . . . Well . . . My . . ."

"God takes his time," I say.

"Yes, he does," says Granny.

⊹ ⊹ ⊹

Mama comes home and says tomorrow I should read Exodus, but I tell her I'd rather keep on learning about Noah's ark, right up to the puppet show. "Fine," she says. She's happy I ain't complaining.

✠ ✠ ✠

Wednesday night we all drive over to Remnant. Granny brings a rhubarb pie. We walk down to the church basement, and I put Mrs. Noah on the bench behind the puppet stage.

Then who should walk in with Sister Coates but Pastor and Mrs. Tilbury.

"They was on their way back to Oklahoma, so I said come for the potluck," says Sister Coates.

I get in the food line. There's fried chicken, meat loaf, tuna-noodle casserole, sloppy joes, three kinds of salad, and six kinds of pie.

The Noah's ark backdrop that me and Chester was supposed to use is up on the bulletin board.

"Where was you last Sunday?" says Chester, getting in line behind me.

"Busy," I say. "Where was you the week before?"

Chester puts his hand on his chest and coughs. He sets with his mama.

I set with Jed Bean and Chloe.

Once everybody has their food, Sister Coates goes up to the podium and raises her hand. "Lord bless this food to our bodies and guide us as we partake in family fellowship. In Jesus' name."

"Amen!"

✠ ✠ ✠

Brother Lucas announces that all kids working on the puppet show should come backstage as soon as possible.

Me, Jed, and Chloe finish dinner, drop our plates in the waste can, and head back.

Chester and Orlin's already there. I make sure all the backdrops is in order and pull down black for Day One.

Brother Lucas's forehead's all beaded up with sweat. Looks like Karo syrup.

Jonathan Safer comes on back.

"All right," says Brother Lucas. "I'm a-going out when Sister Coates introduces me. You just set tight."

We hear everyone rearranging the tables and chairs, getting the folding chairs lined up in rows.

Sister Coates leads everyone in singing "Blest Be the Tie That Binds." Then she says, "I'd like to bring out Brother

Lucas. He's been a-working with the juniors on their puppet play of the Creation."

Brother Lucas slips out between the church curtain and the puppet theatre. He clears his throat. "We learned a lot about the Bible doing this. Plus the juniors made this here stage, made their own puppets, too. We had a real good time. Hope you like it." He comes back.

I open the curtains.

Orlin Coates does his "Being the Supreme Being" speech. He divides the light from the dark and pulls the firmament out of the waters. Everything's fine until I pull down a backdrop.

Clunk-clunk-clunk-clunk-clunk-clunk-clunk.

We can hear people laughing.

Orlin looks at me.

"I didn't do nothing," I whisper.

Orlin goes on, creating and proclaiming, but each time I roll down a backdrop, we hear the audience laugh. It's like God went clunk-clunk-clunk-clunk-clunk every time he made a new day.

Me and the other kids is laughing, too.

"God ain't funny," Orlin whispers.

"Quiet!" says Brother Lucas. He waves his hand at us.

Orlin makes his Day Six speech, then Chloe's Eve

comes out. The audience hoots and hollers. Chloe don't mind. She struts that Eve around like a princess. Besides them titties, she's give Eve a big red hair ribbon.

Her, Jed, and Jonathan do Temptation; then I shut the curtains. We take away all the backdrops but the cheesecloth.

Chester's standing on one side, and I'm on the other. Chloe opens the curtains. I can see the whole audience, right through the cheesecloth. Mama's setting there with Daddy and Granny. Sister Coates is a-setting in the front row with Pastor and Mrs. Tilbury.

We first make like the ark's bobbing in heavy seas, up and down, up and down. Then we just start talking.

"Mr. Noah," I say, "we got some problems."

"What kind of problems?" says Noah.

"All them animals is seasick, Mr. Noah, and the place stinks to high Heaven."

"Open up the windows," says Noah.

"Mr. Noah, you only made one."

"That's what the Lord told me to do."

"Well, the Lord don't have to live on this boat. He should have told you to make more windows. Truth is, Mr. Noah, them animals need their cages cleaned out."

Mr. Noah sighs. "Mrs. Noah, I'm getting sick and tired of your complaining. How about you and the wives tending to them cages."

"Mr. Noah, this ark is a-carrying twenty thousand animals. We got ten thousand cages on three levels. Each of them cages stink, and a Komodo dragon's running loose. Now me and the girls ain't a-going down there."

"Why not just hose it down?"

"Mr. Noah, we ain't got no hoses. We need shovels and we need buckets. I hope you remembered to bring them things because the smell is bad. You know what a kitty box can smell like, Mr. Noah, when it ain't been cleaned. Now we got some mighty big animals, and they's using their cage for a litter box. Mr. Noah, you ever seen how much a T. rex poops? Plus we got two hippos, two elephants, two rhinos, and a bunch of other beasts, all of them making their own mess."

"Mrs. Noah," says Mr. Noah, "you're nothing but a fussbudget."

"And you're nothing but a lazy old man."

Right then Brother Lucas has Chloe drop down a bird with a leaf in its mouth. Means the waters is going down. I know Brother Lucas wants to end this show real quick.

Orlin comes on. "I DO SET A RAINBOW IN THE CLOUD AND DO PROMISE THAT I WILL NEVER AGAIN FLOOD THIS HERE EARTH. AMEN."

So we's all cheering, Chloe shuts them curtains, and that's the end of the puppet show.

We all come out onstage, Orlin still complaining to Brother Lucas that people was laughing at God.

I don't even look at Mama. She's probably thinking I've been taken over by the Devil.

But everyone applauds and applauds, especially Pastor Tilbury. He's slapping his feet together like a seal.

Him and Mrs. Tilbury come up. "Well I loved your Mrs. Noah," says Mrs. Tilbury. "Made me think, it did. How in Heaven's name did they manage on that ark? Must have been some trick to it, eight people tending ten thousand cages."

"I think them animals was hypnotized," says Pastor Tilbury.

"Or maybe they was all in hibernation," says Mrs. Tilbury.

"But not all animals hibernate," I say.

"Mary Mae, you got a good questioning mind," says Pastor Tilbury.

"Mary Mae's studying at home now," says Sister Coates.

Mama steps in, proud to tell the story. "I did not like what they was teaching, so I pulled her out of school. Told them, 'You can keep your books, I want my daughter brought up Bible.'"

"They was teaching about fossils," says Daddy, "but

we got fossils in our own backyard. It don't seem right to keep Mary Mae from looking at 'em. What do you think, Pastor Tilbury?"

"I can understand your concern," he says to Mama, "but fossils is God's creatures, too. Nothing wrong with fossils. I collect them myself. Got me some crinoids and brachiopods. The way I see it, they was all fossilized during Noah's flood in 3500 B.C."

"Now me, I believe they was fossilized in 90,000 B.C.," says Mrs. Tilbury. "I believe the world is a hundred thousand years old."

"I think you're way off," Pastor Tilbury says to his wife, "but everyone's got a right to their opinion."

Imagine that. A man of the Lord saying you got a right to your opinion.

I start to give mine, but Granny raps my leg with her cane.

"I say dig all the fossils you want," says Pastor Tilbury. "They's proof of God's early Creation."

"Do you mean the Lord ain't trying to trick us?" says Mama.

"Fossils is mentioned right in the Bible," says Pastor Tilbury. "'For the invisible things of him from the Creation.' I think it's Romans."

Seeing as how fossils is okay, I tell all. "We seen a whole riverbed full of fossils last weekend," I say.

Even Mama chimes in. "Yes, we did," she says. "Down in Clarksville at the Falls of the Ohio. Beautiful fossils. Now I won't feel so wicked that I looked at them."

I'm feeling grace now, like the Lord's got his arm wrapped around us all, standing here in this circle. Mama's feeling it, too. "Mary Mae," she says, "I believe the Lord wants you back in school. And I'm sorry. I oughtn't to have acted so quickly." Tears is running down Mama's cheeks, and she hugs me, and I'm crying and hugging her back.

"You got a real smart little girl there," says Pastor Tilbury.

"I know it," says Mama.

But I got to ask Mama one important thing. "Can I have my fossil collection?"

"Long as you keep it dusted," she says.

"I'll make you a shelf," says Daddy.

17.
Blessed

Mama takes me back to school Thursday morning.

We walk into Mr. Trimble's office. "Mrs. Krebs," he says, and puts out his hand.

"I'm sorry I took Mary Mae out of school," says Mama. "I acted too hastily. Last night we had a guest pastor at the church that says it's all right to dig up fossils."

"You can learn a lot from them," says Mr. Trimble. "We're pleased to have Mary Mae back." He says he'll gather my books for me and I can go on up to class.

Miss Sizemore's setting on the far side of the room beside a papier maché glacier. "You're back!" she shrieks. Everybody's cheering.

Herschel shows me some pebbles he's brought in for a glacial moraine.

✠ ✠ ✠

Sunday at church, me and Granny sing a song we wrote together—"Holy Father Bring Me Joy." Everybody's a-clapping on the chorus. It's Granny's last Sunday here. Her blood's down, the doctor says, so she can go back home.

We set down, and Sister Coates asks who would like to give thanks.

Jonathan Safer says his uncle's helping him build a racer for the Soap Box Derby.

"Hallelujah! Praise the Lord!"

Wilma Tatters says, "Hallelujah, I got me a brand-new Exercycle."

I stand up. "I'm grateful my granny's been here with us for these last two months. And we've had so many good times."

"Praise the Lord! Hallelujah!"

✠ ✠ ✠

Sister Coates preaches on the Beatitudes, all them "blesseds." Blessed are the meek, for they shall inherit the earth. Blessed are the pure in heart, for they shall see God. Blessed are the merciful, for they shall obtain mercy. She runs through the whole list, explaining each one. It's like a list of playground rules, only you don't get just a rule, you get a blessing and a promise.

Now I ain't all them things, that's for sure. I ain't meek, because I'm always asking questions. But I am pure in heart. At least I try to be. And with Granny going next week, I hope to be comforted. I got my guitar and Granny's music. I got Mrs. Noah setting on my dressing table, and I got my fossils all lined up on a shelf Daddy made for me that's hanging on the wall. I'm always adding to it, and I keep it dusted because Mama wants it clean up there.

Since 1988, the time of this story, three museums within the Cincinnati–northern Kentucky–southern Indiana area have opened.

To see trilobites and other Ordovician fossils, visitors may tour the following sites:

The Cincinnati Museum Center at Union Terminal
1301 Western Avenue
Cincinnati, Ohio

and

The Falls of the Ohio State Park Interpretive Center
201 West Riverside Drive
Clarksville, Indiana

When the river is low, visitors may walk over the fossil beds just as Mary Mae did.

To view exhibits that depict the earth as no more than six thousand years old, visitors may tour the following site:

The Creation Museum
2800 Bullittsburg Church Road
Petersburg, Kentucky

Acknowledgments

My deepest gratitude to the following:

My parents, Henry and Jeanne Hipkins, who long ago read my sisters and me the Old Testament Bible stories.

My husband, Wayne Sheridan, maker of gourmet dinners and always First Listener. And my sons, Dominic and Maxwell.

Mary Pinkham, Betty Hughes, and Pat Brunell, Boothbay Harbor librarians. And to Barbara House and Diane Dorbin, library program directors. I thank you for all your help and enthusiasm.

Jane Randall, former children's librarian at the Crescent Hill Public Library in Louisville, Kentucky, who left us far too soon.

My editor, Erica Zappy, who believed in Mary Mae from the start.

My agent, Jennie Dunham, and fellow writers Amy MacDonald, Robin MacCready, Karen Allen, and Patricia Murray. Also Rebecca Bond at Houghton Mifflin. Wonderful readers, all. And Kirsten Cappy, a great fan of trilobites.

Glenn Storrs, director of Science Research and Withrow Farny Curator of Vertebrate Paleontology at the Cincinnati Museum Center. When I asked Dr. Storrs where one might dig for fossils in Norwood, Ohio, he said, "If you can find a construction site or road cut anywhere it should be hopping with fossils. Norwood, like Cincinnati, will be rich in Ordovician fossils wherever the bedrock is exposed."

And Marjorie Behrman, my fifth grade teacher, who showed me where the Ohio River used to flow.